GOING IN DEEP

NEW YORK TIMES BESTSELLING AUTHOR

CARLY PHILLIPS

Billionaire Bad Boys: Rich, Powerful and sexy as hell.
All Billionaire Bad Boys Novels stand alone!

He isn't Mr. Nice Guy…

Julian Dane thought he'd hit rock bottom—until he met a woman (isn't that what they all say?). He used her and broke her heart. Now he wants to turn things around but the damage he dealt stands in his way.

Kendall Parker's unique issues have made it hard to live a normal life. Very few people understand her and she trusts even less … but she believed in Julian once, and he only betrayed her.

Now Julian is back—a new man—and determined to win Kendall's heart. But this reformed bad boy just might find that Going in Deep is harder than it looks.

"Carly Phillips is synonymous with red-hot romance and passionate love."
—Lauren Blakely, NY Times Bestselling Author

* * *

Chapter One

A MAN DIDN'T make mistakes. He made choices. Bad ones stayed with him for a long time but, with a little luck and a lot of hard work, hopefully not forever. With planning and diligence, he could make amends. And that had been Julian Dane's blueprint for how to live his life for the last two hundred and seventy days.

He'd been clean and off drugs for way longer, but the time since he'd acted like a lowlife dirtbag and hurt an innocent woman haunted him more than his past addiction. So he counted his sobriety from that day on. The day he'd decided to act like a decent human being, make amends, and truly change.

He walked out of his Alcoholics Anonymous meeting, his close friend and sponsor by his side. He'd tried Narcotics Anonymous, but at the suggestion of his old therapist, he'd related more to the people in the A.A. meetings, their twelve-step program suiting his needs—beginning with admitting he was powerless over his addiction, including making apologies and amends, and ending with practicing everything he'd learned in all his affairs. And everything in between.

"You up for dinner?" Nick Cantone, his sponsor, asked.

They often caught a bite after a meeting.

"I told Lauren I wouldn't be home until later, so she's grabbing something to eat with friends," he said, referring to his wife.

Julian's empty stomach grumbled in agreement. "Sure," he said with a grin.

They headed for a small diner on the corner, a typical New York City haunt, and chose an empty booth, sitting across from each other on the plastic seats. Julian didn't need to look at the laminated menus. A burger and fries would suit him fine. The waiter poured them water and took their orders.

They sat in silence for a few minutes. Neither man spoke about what went on inside a meeting unless Julian brought it up first. And though he was feeling pensive, he wasn't in the mood to talk about his past. He wasn't currently struggling with sobriety, didn't miss the pull of drugs. There had been a time he'd self-medicated as an escape, and he had lost himself for a while. He had his shit together now but didn't kid himself. A slip was always possible, so he worked the program.

"So I was thinking," Nick said as Julian picked up a glass of water and took a drink, "it's time you got back into the dating game. I want to introduce you to a woman I work with. I think you two would hit it off. I happen to know she's looking for a decent guy. And if you're not interested in a relationship, I know another chick who's more into a no-strings hookup."

Julian raised an eyebrow in surprise. "You playing matchmaker now?"

A grin split Nick's face. "No. I just happened to overhear water cooler conversation at the office." Nick owned a real estate company, and Julian had no doubt he heard his fair share of gossip.

"I'm too busy to worry about dating." Julian's free-lance cyber security business was picking up. He'd hired outside contractors and things were finally going well. He wanted to keep his focus where it belonged.

"Next thing I know you'll tell me your hand is working just fine," Nick muttered.

Julian rolled his eyes. Everyone thought they were a comedian.

Although he'd be the first to admit he did give his hand a workout considering he wasn't currently dating and hadn't had a hookup, as Nick called it, in a while. He could date the last time he'd buried himself between a woman's sweet thighs, but that would lead him to think about her. And that train of thought always led nowhere.

"Jesus," he said to Nick, annoyed with where the

conversation had taken him. "I'm... not ready to date... or fuck. I have loose ends I have to tie up, and until I do that, I'm not getting involved with anyone else."

Julian had apologies left to make, one in particular, which brought him back to thoughts of *her*—and he couldn't get near Kendall Parker to have his say. He'd tried, but her brother-in-law, and Julian's one-time best friend, Kaden Barnes, wouldn't let him close.

Not that Julian blamed him. Julian and Kade had a nasty history, made worse by Julian's addiction and piss-poor choices. You didn't sue an old friend, drag up his hidden, ugly past, use his sister-in-law, and walk away unscathed. Julian had done all those things. And more. But Kade didn't know the man Julian was now, how hard he'd fought to put the past behind him and move forward.

Nick studied him thoughtfully, so Julian did the same in return. His friend was in his late forties, to Julian's thirty, his hair starting to gray, and he'd been clean and sober for over ten years. They'd met at Julian's first meeting and bonded over burgers and stories afterwards.

Nick had taken Julian into his family, invited Julian and his sister over for holidays, and he generally boosted Julian up. He believed in him. Much like Kade had once done, except now Julian was smarter and more receptive to help and friendship.

Sometimes it seemed like Julian's thoughts always came back to Kaden Barnes and Kendall Parker.

"It's time for you to talk to her," Nick said, all but reading his mind. "You can't move on with your life until you settle the past."

"I know." Julian wrapped his hand around the cold glass of ice water. "I just don't want to upset the delicate balance of *her* life." And concern about another human being instead of his own was a novel emotion for Julian.

The only person he'd ever put first was his younger sister. Alyssa was the driving force behind every move Julian had made. Good and bad. Not that he'd ever use her as an excuse for his addiction or behavior. He had family history and genetics at work, and his own shitty choices to thank for that. But Alyssa's accident had altered the course of Julian's life. That was something he couldn't deny.

"You don't know you'll upset Kendall's life. Just because Kade told you to stay away doesn't mean he knows what's best for her. Maybe she needs closure as much as you do," Nick said.

That Kendall might need to see him, too, wasn't something Julian had considered before. He ran a hand over his face, rubbing his tired eyes.

"Maybe you have a point," Julian conceded, and

thought about Kendall Parker.

She was a beautiful, vibrant woman, who, for a brief time, had been a light in his self-created dark life. Only he'd been too stupid to appreciate her. He'd also been so wrapped up in his quest for revenge and getting what he'd believed was rightfully his share of Kade and his partners' company, Blink, Julian had been blind to the woman right in front of him. Kendall had been in as much trouble as he'd been.

She lived with bipolar disorder and Julian hadn't known. She had her own life challenges, something, looking back, he could have at least noticed during their time together. Instead he'd been mindless to anything but his own needs. He'd used her for personal gain, pitted her against her twin and Kade, and generally fucked up her life.

His stomach twisted painfully at the reminder. "What if she's gotten her shit together?" he asked Nick. "What if seeing me sends her spiraling?" He couldn't live with himself.

Nick pointed a fork his way. "Doesn't she need to be responsible for her behavior just like you need to own yours?" his friend countered, spouting what sounded like group tenets.

He wasn't wrong.

With a groan, Julian leaned his arms on the linoleum tabletop. "I don't know where she lives or works."

He knew where she'd resided last year, but she might have moved.

"Bullshit excuses."

Julian could always count on Nick to call him out.

"All you probably need to do is check Facebook. Or put those tech skills of yours to good use. I'm sure you can catch up with her when her watchdog brother-in-law isn't around."

At the thought of seeing Kendall again, a mixture of heady anticipation combined with sheer nerves kicked in.

"I'll consider it," Julian promised.

And it was all he thought about for the next few days. Days he spent wrestling with his conscience. He hadn't had much of one before Kendall, but his sense of morals was more developed now, as it should have been all along.

Apparently it had taken one brown-haired, blue-eyed vixen to get under his skin, make him look in the mirror and come to terms with the man he'd become.

He owed her an apology. Whether her family liked it or not.

★　★　★

WITH MUSIC PLAYING in the background, Kendall Parker nodded her head to the beat as she counted out the brightly colored pills she took daily. She was careful as she filled the plastic holder that was labeled by individual days and divided by a.m. and p.m. doses, as prescribed by her therapist. In a separate vial, she included her daily antianxiety medication, also doctor-approved.

She clicked each case shut tight, then left the plastic containers next to the cookie jar in the kitchen, where they were visible so she wouldn't forget. Not that she would. She hadn't skipped a dose since she'd come home from her in-treatment stay at Maple Hill a little over a year ago.

Her dog, Waffles, a small terrier mix she'd adopted during one of her manic phases, jumped up and down, begging for a treat.

"No. You just had one, sweet girl," Kendall said, bending to pat the tan fluffy dog on the head.

Waffles had turned into a fabulous emotional-support dog. She offered Kendall comfort and eased her anxiety. Petting the soft fur soothed her. A lick reassured her.

Kendall lived with bipolar I disorder and now that she was on the right medication, along with a steady diet of therapy, life was good and looking better every day, the mistakes and hurts of last year behind her. She was lucky her twin sister, Lexie, and brother-in-law, Kade, were kind enough to forgive and forget, because her family meant everything to Kendall.

She changed from her pajamas into an old pair of jeans and a gray tee shirt with her oldest pair of sneakers. Since she worked as a dog walker for a growing number of clients and held a steady job at For Paws, a not-for-profit animal shelter in Midtown Manhattan, it was guaranteed she'd be dealing with animal fur and poop. No reason for nice clothing in her day job.

She glanced at her watch, calculating her time before the next bus headed downtown. It was too warm to take the subway. She lived on the Upper East Side, courtesy of her father, who'd bought the apartment for Lexie and Kendall—when Lexie had all but been her twin's caretaker. Kendall wasn't earning enough to pay rent, but she was self-sufficient in many other ways.

All huge progress.

Lexie and Kade had married and Lexie moved into Kade's place, and Kendall wanted her father to sell this two-bedroom so she could move into something smaller. He preferred that she stay here and have extra room. That was her father, always compensating. For Kendall's illness. For her mother's debilitating depression.

She pushed those thoughts away. Focused on the present. Reminded herself of all the good things in her life, of which there were many. Don't dwell on the negative or the things she couldn't change.

"Hey, Waffles. I'll be back during lunch to walk you, okay?"

The pup looked up at Kendall with big brown eyes that said, *Don't leave me.* In an attempt to make her feel worse, the dog then lay down, her head on her front paws, with a heavy sigh.

"Goofball. I always come back." Kendall blew her a kiss and headed out the door for work.

A short while later, she walked into For Paws, the back of her neck damp from the unseasonable June heat, despite the fact that she'd tied her hair into a high ponytail to keep herself cool.

"Hi, Josie. What's up this beautiful day?" Kendall tossed her backpack onto the floor beneath the desk she occupied when she wasn't working in the back with the dogs in their crates or runs.

Josie Dawson, her boss, was a pretty brunette who'd taken a risk hiring a woman with no employment history. Josie had urgently needed to fill the paid position, and Kendall had been equally desperate for a job. Any job. Kendall had proven herself to be reliable, and the job fulfilled a very basic need of feeling self-sufficient. The other woman didn't realize it, but Kendall owed Josie a lot for giving her a chance.

Josie was the first *friend* Kendall had made on her own in years. One that wasn't connected to her sister.

Kendall had a bad habit of pushing people away, her highs and lows too much for most to handle. The new and improved Kendall—the properly medicated Kendall—lived life on a more even keel, which enabled her to make and keep both her job and her friend.

"How's Steve?" she asked of the pit mix that was small for his age and had been in the kennel for way too long. The one bad thing about Kendall's position was that she couldn't bring all the dogs home with her. Because she really wanted to.

"He's good," Josie said. "He ate today. He just really needs a loving home." But people were afraid to take chances on pitties, no matter how little the mix of genetics.

The breed had a bad reputation but Kendall didn't care. She'd fallen for Steve, named by the person who'd dumped him at the shelter when training became too hard. She'd have taken him home, but Kendall's building rules allowed for only one dog, so she had to leave her heart here every night. It was probably a good thing or she'd end up being the crazy lady who hoarded dogs. All she could do was spend the day giving otherwise abandoned dogs all the love, cuddles, and talking to that she could, in the limited time she was there.

"I'll take him for a walk in a little while and spend some time with them all."

"Sounds good," Josie said. "I left some paperwork on the desk for you."

Kendall nodded and got to work. The morning passed quickly, and before she knew it, lunch was fast approaching. She'd brought a cup of yogurt and fruit to eat at her desk, but first she wanted to finish up the filing.

Kendall bent over a metal cabinet, putting away the paperwork for recent adoptions, while Josie was in the back, showing a family the available dogs.

The sound of the front door chimes caught Kendall's attention. "I'll be right with you," she called without looking up.

"Take your time," a familiar masculine voice said, and Kendall's hand froze midair.

She lowered the papers, dropping them on top of the cabinet, and slowly rose to her feet, her heart slamming against her chest, a million beats a second.

She turned to face Julian, immediately struck by his good looks, as she was every time she laid eyes on the man. They'd first met at the gym, and she'd been captivated by his dark hair, green eyes, and sexy smile—completely unaware he'd already known who she was and that he had been setting her up the whole time he'd been sweet-talking her into his clutches.

Today his dark hair was cut short, his facial scruff a hot, sexy addition to his overall good looks. He wore a pair of faded jeans that molded to his strong thighs, a black tee shirt, his forearm muscles bunching from beneath the short sleeves, and a pair of leather bracelets she didn't remember on his right wrist.

His overall appearance was casual, sexy ... and wary, if the expression in his eyes was anything to go by. But she didn't trust anything she saw at a glance. Not when it came to Julian Dane.

He studied her, her body heating as his gaze raked over her. She didn't look her best, didn't have to for the job she held, but she straightened her shoulders, meeting his gaze. As if she hadn't thought about him in ages. Which wasn't true. She hadn't *let* herself think about him, cutting off any wayward slips he made into her consciousness.

Nobody had done as much damage in her life as Julian, mostly because she'd cared so much and he'd used her feelings for him against her. She was determined to handle him with the cool detachment he deserved.

"What are you doing here?" she asked, amazed her voice sounded calm and composed.

"I wanted to see you."

His smooth, deep voice washed over her, better memories of their time together warring with the knowledge of his real intentions. He'd wined her, dined her, and the sex between them had been incredible. She'd fallen for him hard, appreciating how he'd enjoyed her highs, not realizing he was doing more damage by encouraging her erratic behavior.

"I have nothing to say to you, Julian. Go away." She picked up the still-to-be-filed papers with shaking hands.

He stepped up to the desk, and she was grateful for the barrier between them, but it didn't prevent her from catching a whiff of his masculine scent and familiar, woodsy cologne.

She swallowed hard, forcing away memories of his hands on her body, gliding up her thighs, over her sex, bringing her to an intense orgasm.

"I've tried to talk to you a couple of times." He spoke, unaware of her inappropriate thoughts. "Kade and Lexie haven't let me get near you."

Kendall narrowed her gaze at what sounded like an accusation against her twin and her husband. "Don't you think there's good reason for that?"

A muscle ticked in his jaw, the only indication her words hurt him. "Give me five minutes. Please."

"I'm working."

"After work, then."

She shook her head. "I have an appointment." Therapy, the subject of which he'd just altered by showing his face here and forcing her to think about him again.

"After your appointment?"

When she didn't immediately answer, he went on. "Lunch today? Tomorrow?"

She scowled at his persistence, frustrated with herself because she was curious about what he had to say. But she wasn't ready to give in, mostly because she didn't trust herself to be alone with him.

"How about a cup of coffee any time you choose?" he tried again.

"Careful, Julian. I might think you're desperate."

"What makes you think I'm not?" He settled a hip on her desk, clearly digging in, refusing to leave until he got the answer he desired. "Okay, you won't just agree to talk to me. I get that and I understand why."

She knew better than to feel relieved. He was merely biding his time. Still, she had to try and push him further. "So you'll give up and go home?"

He flinched at her words but remained in place, his steady gaze on hers. "Not so fast, kitten."

"Don't call me that." It was too intimate, too much. He'd had his reasons for the nickname he'd bestowed on her, and today they made her blush. She folded her arms across her chest, protecting her heavily beating heart.

He blew out a long breath. "I guess you're going to make me spell it out right here, right now. I'm in Alcoholics Anonymous—works for me better than

Narcotics Anonymous," he said, the same muscle ticking at the corner of his eye as he admitted a truth she hadn't seen coming.

She gripped the edge of her desk with both hands.

"I'm seriously working the program, and I want to talk to you. There are things I need to say," he said, his voice low, his tone sincere.

Raw honesty was the last thing she'd expected to hear from him, and her heart twisted, softening toward him. How could it not? She'd done the therapy thing herself. Had gone through apologies with her sister, Kade, and her father, taking responsibility for her actions. Never mind that Julian had instigated some of her behavior, she'd made her own decisions. So she understood his need to apologize to her now.

But if she let him in in any way, she'd be risking the trust her sister and her husband placed in her. They wanted her to steer clear of Julian, and they had good, solid reasons for their feelings.

Reasons she agreed with herself. And she couldn't justify hearing him out for any reason other than she was weak when it came to Julian Dane.

"I'm sorry," she said, the words painful but necessary. "But I can't. If you need to apologize," which she knew was a tenet of his program, "then know that I hear you. And I appreciate the sentiment." She could at least give him that.

Disappointment flashed across his handsome features, and she felt bad. "That's not all I have to say."

She swallowed hard, fighting past the need to listen to what he wanted to tell her. She couldn't let it matter. "You need to hear me, Julian. Go home."

"Okay." He rose from his seat on the desk, both shocking and disappointing her with his sudden acquiescence.

Before she could blink, she watched his back as he strode out the door, giving her exactly what she had asked for. And leaving her feeling emptier than she could have imagined.

Chapter Two

To Kendall's surprise, Julian showed up at the shelter the next day, again asking to talk. This time, the place was busy with people picking up already signed-for and adopted animals, families looking at potential pets, and a devastated woman who had to leave her beloved dog because the women's shelter she was living in didn't allow her to keep him.

Kendall was fried and exhausted, and the last thing she could deal with was a sexy-as-sin Julian, waiting patiently for her to have time for him.

Thank goodness he realized the day wasn't going to lighten up, and he disappeared during one of her trips to the kennels in the back. Once again, she ignored the immense feeling of disappointment she experienced at his leaving, reminding herself it was for the best. In fact, if he gave up, he'd be doing her a favor.

The next day, there was no sign of Julian, and Kendall spent the morning with the animals. She was worried about one pup in particular. Monty, a mix of too many breeds to count, with big brown eyes, wasn't feeling well. The vet who donated his time was coming to check him over this afternoon. Kendall cleaned his crate and spoke to him gently, promising he'd feel better soon. He curled up in the corner of his crate and looked at her with soulful eyes, breaking her heart.

She checked on the other dogs and spent a few minutes with Steve before washing her hands and walking into the front office, where Josie manned the desk.

"I'm glad the vet's coming for Monty," Kendall said. "The poor guy's stomach is really bad." Her words trailed off as she caught sight of Julian, his head bent over a form as he filled out paperwork.

"What's going on?" she asked, her gaze flying from him to Josie.

"Mr. Dane—"

"Julian," he said, glancing up and flashing Josie his most endearing smile.

"Julian," Josie said obligingly, "wants to adopt."

"What? Since when?" Kendall asked.

Josie's eyes opened wide at her harsh tone. "Kendall!"

"That's okay. We know each other," Julian said. "And I'm sure I'm surprising Kendall. But the truth is I work from home. I'm around most of the day. It's lonely and I've been wanting a pet for a while. Coming here to talk to you just pushed the idea to the forefront of my mind."

Kendall narrowed her gaze, uncertain of his sudden decision. "You need two references," she said, wondering if the process would deter him.

He shrugged. "Not a problem."

"A dog is a lifetime commitment. Are you sure you want a pet and not an excuse to come here?" She had to ask.

He placed the pen down and folded his arms across his broad chest. "One hundred percent certain."

From her seat at the desk, Kendall felt Josie's shocked gaze following their conversation.

"We don't do same-day adoptions," Kendall went on, explaining their rules.

He shrugged. "I'll come back tomorrow."

He had an answer for everything. And his gaze never left hers.

"Did you pick out a pet?" She hadn't seen him in the back, but then she'd been up to her elbows in dog diarrhea.

"I was just about to ask you to walk him back and show him around," Josie said. "I have an appointment with Madeline Ostrasky." The shelter's biggest donor.

Which meant Kendall would have to be the one to escort Julian around. She shot him a glare, annoyed, though it wasn't his fault they'd been paired up. He couldn't have been certain she'd be the one he ended up working with.

He might want a pet, but she had a feeling if he hadn't gotten to see her today, he'd just have shown up again. And again. For some reason, he'd decided the time had come to be persistent.

Which meant she was going to have to listen to what he had to say. "Come on," Kendall said. "I'll show you our pups."

He followed her out back, and she stopped short, wanting to hear his thoughts before she showed him the dogs. "Do you have any idea what kind of dog you're looking for? Big? Small? Are you still in your one-bedroom? There's not much room there for a bigger dog," she said before he could formulate a reply.

He grinned at her overzealousness. "I just want a companion dog. One I can take on walks and one who'll be just as happy hanging around when I have to work."

"Are you sure—"

"Kendall." He cut her off. "I know what I want." His gaze zeroed in on hers, his dual meaning clear.

His want extended to her, as well, and her entire body trembled in reaction, her nipples puckering beneath her tee shirt.

"Okay. Let's walk through," she said, quickly turning away. She bypassed the larger dogs, the ones who needed room to run, and slowed when she approached the runs with the small- to medium-size dogs, standing back so he could look without her interference. "Just ask if you have any questions."

"Thank you." He walked back and forth, pausing at different dogs, talking to them over the barking that inevitably ensued just by virtue of their presence.

He paused by Monty's crate. "Is he okay?" he asked of the dog lying in the corner.

"His stomach is upset. The vet's coming this afternoon. I'm worried about him," she admitted. "His name's Monty."

"Hey, boy. Monty, come here." Julian knelt down, but the mixed breed wasn't moving.

Julian moved on, going back and forth between a few dogs before stopping by Steve's pen. "Him." He pointed at the gray puppy. "Can I go in and see him?"

Her heart skipped a beat, torn by her feelings. Happy someone was interested in her boy and sad because if Julian picked Steve to adopt and took him home, she'd never see him again.

She swallowed hard and opened the door with her key. "This is Steve," she said as they entered, and the dog with the weird floppy ears jumped up to greet them. "He's a pit mix, which has made his adoption difficult. Families don't tend to want pit bulls."

"But look at that face." Julian knelt down so he

was eye level with the dog, who proceeded to sniff him all over. Julian patiently waited, giving Steve time to become familiar with his scent. "So it's Steve?" he asked, confirming the name.

"Yes. His owner said he had problems training him and left him here, but to be honest, he's been a great dog from day one. I walk the dogs, and I can tell you he's easy to train, picks up commands quickly, and wants to please."

She petted his head, bending down beside Julian. Steve put his head on her knee.

"I know. You're a good boy," she crooned to him.

He let out a small whine.

Julian studied her with the dog, his gaze steady and too damned perceptive. She had a feeling he could see her heart and how much she adored this particular pup.

"You recommend him?" he asked.

"Yeah," she said over the lump in her throat. "He's two years old, full size, seems good with the other dogs, and he has an easygoing personality."

"Sounds like my dog," Julian said in a gruff but happy voice.

She rose to her feet, leaning against the chain enclosure. "I'll leave you two alone for a little while. Make sure you have time with him. You know, so you're certain he's the one you want."

Julian settled on the kennel floor, not at all worried about dirt. Steve immediately nuzzled up to his chest, and Kendall withheld a soft sigh.

"There's no need for you to leave. I'm sure," Julian said, chuckling, his big hand stroking the dog's flat fur.

She blew out a long breath, shaken that the dog she'd considered her boy would be going home with Julian, of all people. Well, she'd prayed Steve would get a home, and now he had one.

"Okay, well, you can leave the adoption fee, which is refundable if things don't work out. We'll need to check your references, and you can take the time to stock up on everything you'll need for owning a pet. We have a list we'll give you. Assuming everything checks out, you can come back for him tomorrow."

"Hear that, Steve? Only one more night in this place."

Steve seemed to understand, licking Julian's face with his big tongue.

It took awhile for Julian to leave the pen. Like Kendall, he'd already bonded with Steve. Finally, he stepped out, and Kendall locked the run once more, then led Julian back out front.

For the next few minutes, he filled out the rest of the paperwork, left his references, and paid the adoption fee.

It wasn't until after he left that Kendall realized he

hadn't offered up the apology or tried to talk to her about anything other than pet adoption, leaving her feeling strangely off-balance. And uncertain about what his intentions would be when he saw her again.

★ ★ ★

JULIAN WASN'T PLAYING games. He wasn't adopting a dog in order to get close to Kendall. With the responsibility he was taking on, that would be sheer insanity. At a local pet store, he purchased a leash and collar, a crate, food bowls, and other things he'd need for his new friend, Steve.

What kind of name was Steve for a dog? He felt like he was bringing home a real roommate with that name. But he'd felt the pull toward the dog from the minute he looked into the pup's soulful eyes.

Julian worked long hours in his apartment, and a dog would force him out of the house to take breaks and walks, and provide him with much-needed company. So the dog was a real want in his life, even if seeing Kendall at her job had given him the push he needed to make it happen.

And he wasn't withholding his apology to Kendall on purpose. It's just that when he'd walked into the back room with Kendall, he'd been struck hard by how different she seemed now from the woman he'd known. This Kendall Parker was low-key, diligent about her job, serious about the dogs and, it seemed, about life.

When he'd seen her last, she'd been ebullient, bubbly, and on a normal day, she was bouncing up and down while she talked. She'd been, during the time they were together, on a constant high. She talked fast, and often he had trouble keeping up, but she was so happy it was impossible for her good mood not to rub off on him.

She'd suggested a late-night ride to the top of the Empire State Building, no fear of heights or reason given.

As a result, he'd suggest impulsive trips just to keep up. Blowing off work for a drive upstate, accompanying her on excessive shopping trips. She hadn't needed much sleep, and on the nights he was with her, he'd learned to function on less.

He'd also discovered she loved sex. Risky sex. A lot of sex. And he'd been too blinded and wrapped up in Kendall to see through to her problems. All he had to do was think back and remember, and his entire body came alive. There was something about Kendall that got to him, and it wasn't just because she was a sex kitten.

For a little while, she'd been *his* kitten. He placed a hand over his hard cock, adjusting himself as he stared out the window of his apartment, unable to focus on work. This new and, he had to believe, improved Kendall intrigued him. She was a woman of substance, something that had been there all along, but she'd buried the seriousness beneath a manic episode. He just wished he'd known.

Why? Because he'd been such a decent guy? He'd have gotten her help? He shook his head, pushing away the self-loathing that resulted when he acknowledged the answer was no. He would not have.

Julian had changed when he'd discovered he'd used and *hurt* someone who hadn't been in full control of their own actions. While he'd like to believe if he'd known, he'd have stepped up for her, the sad truth was, he probably would not have. Just knowing about her disorder wouldn't have altered his behavior. It was hurting her that had accomplished that feat.

He'd had to hit his own rock bottom before he could rebuild himself.

Just as Kendall had.

He thought of the serious woman in the tight tee shirt, stained with he didn't want to know what. Her long brown hair had been pulled into a high ponytail, swishing sexily as she walked. And her feelings for the dogs pulled at his heart. She clearly felt something strong for the dog he'd chosen… and maybe that was part of the reason he'd been drawn to Steve as well. The pup with the human name was a connection to a woman he still cared about.

One he could no longer get a handle on. So his apology circled around and around in his head and never left his lips. He still intended to talk to Kendall about their past, but to do that, he needed time, and she didn't seem to want to give it to him.

★　★　★

KENDALL TRIED HER best to focus on work and not Julian's renewed presence in her life. As her therapist pointed out, it was a short-term event, something she could handle and put behind her, as she'd done once before. She just needed to get him settled with Steve and he'd be out of her life again, this time for good. She had no desire to question why the thought made her sad or affected her in any way.

From her desk, and at Josie's request, she called Julian's references, starting with his landlord. Julian had already sent over a copy of his lease that included the ability to own a pet.

She didn't know what else she expected to find out, but the man who answered the phone confirmed again that, yes, dogs were allowed in the building and Julian Dane was a model tenant. He paid his rent on time and always had, got along well with his neighbors, had no complaints or warnings leveled against him, and as far as his landlord was concerned, he'd be a responsible pet owner. No red flags there.

Next up was a man named Nick Cantone. He'd known Julian for years, at least according to the adoption form Julian had filled out.

The man answered on the first ring and Kendall introduced herself. "I'm Kendall Parker from For Paws. I'm calling because Julian Dane listed you as a reference. He's interested in adopting one of our dogs."

"Hi, Kendall. Julian told me to expect your call," a friendly-sounding man said.

"I see. Good. Well, I'd just like your overall impressions of Julian. Whether you think he's responsible enough to own a dog, to take care of him, that sort of thing." She tapped her pen against the papers on the desk.

He cleared his throat. "I would say Julian is definitely ready to own a pet. He's... changed a lot in the last year. Grown up. Accepted more responsibility in life."

Kendall narrowed her gaze at the man's pointed comments. If she didn't know better, she'd think Nick was trying to make that point with Kendall personally and as the shelter employee.

"Thank you. I appreciate your time, Mr. Cantone," she said, pleased she'd gotten what she needed.

"Nick, please. After all, I've heard a lot about you,

Kendall," he said, affirming her gut instinct.

Her stomach twisted with unease. "I'm sorry, but I can't say the same thing, and that puts me at a disadvantage."

"I don't want to make you uncomfortable. I just want you to know Julian has worked hard to become a new... a better man."

She swallowed hard. This was supposed to be a dog reference phone call, not one that dug into her old life. "Thank you again for your time. I've gotten all the information I need."

And more that she didn't.

She quickly disconnected the call. Pushing his words aside, she filled out the information on the forms, indicating to Josie she could approve Julian for adoption.

She wasn't ready to ponder anything more. When Julian came for Steve, she'd have to deal with him again. For today, she remained busy with work and kept her mind free of her personal life and her past with Julian Dane.

★ ★ ★

NEW LEASH AND collar in hand, Julian walked into For Paws to pick up his new dog. He was excited to have a pet, happy to know he'd have company, and dammit, looking forward to seeing Kendall again.

When he arrived, she was nowhere to be found. Josie, the other woman he'd met, walked him through the signing of the paperwork, reiterated his responsibilities, and congratulated him on his new family member.

"Are you ready to go get him?" she asked, oblivious to Julian's disappointment in missing out on his chance to see Kendall again.

"Sure thing. Let's go get Steve." He followed her through the back door and into the area where the dogs were kept.

He glanced down the row to Steve's pen, where, to his surprise, Kendall sat with his dog on her lap, petting his head and talking to him in a soft voice.

Julian let out a breath he hadn't been aware of holding, relief and pleasure suffusing him in equal measure. He wouldn't have to leave without talking to Kendall.

"You're going to a good home," Kendall said softly, unaware they were behind her. "You'll be well fed and loved. And even if I won't see you anymore, I'll always remember you."

"It's hard for us not to get attached," Josie explained quietly. "Kendall has a soft spot for Steve because he's been here for such a long time." Josie treated him to a warm smile. "I'll leave you now. Kendall can get you settled from here."

Josie stepped away, heading back to the front office. Julian stood in silence, watching Kendall. Her head was bent low, her long ponytail falling over one shoulder, her neck exposed. The desire to glide his lips over the exposed skin was strong. The urge to mark her there even stronger.

Something about Kendall affected him deeply.

As he quietly walked closer to the pen, once again he was struck by the quiet strength in her now, the even keel to her mood compared to before. He'd known she was smart, but this woman clearly had depths he hadn't seen or plumbed. And he realized how much he wanted to know her again. To learn who she was now and to introduce her to the man he'd become. The one he wanted to be, in part, for her.

At the realization, he blew out a sharp breath.

As if sensing him, she looked up. She stood, the gray dog still in her arms.

He smiled. "Mind if I ask you something?"

"Go on," she said warily.

He took in the protective way she cuddled Steve against her chest. Steve wasn't tiny, and it couldn't have been easy to hold him for long.

"Why didn't you take him? You're obviously bonded," he said as the dog licked her neck. The lucky bastard.

She sighed. "My building has a one-dog-only rule.

And you've met Waffles. Besides, we can't save them all ourselves, as Josie likes to remind me."

He inclined his head. "Then your loss is my gain."

She shifted the dog and held him out for Julian. He accepted his new pet, juggling him with the leash, and held him up, meeting his gaze. "Looks like it's you and me, bud. You ready for your new life?"

Kendall watched them, her gaze softening as she took in the interaction.

"I bought you something," Julian said to the dog, fully aware he was being watched. He bent down and placed the dog on the ground. "Here you go." He hooked the new collar around Steve's neck and backed away, giving him time to adjust.

He shook his head and brushed at the offending collar with his paw, ducking his head at the same time.

"Gotta wear it," Julian said.

"He'll get used to it." Kendall watched the dog and laughed, the sound familiar, welcome, and to his surprise, arousing.

He clearly wasn't over Kendall Parker, despite the fact that he had to be.

"Hook up the leash," she said, oblivious to his thoughts.

He clicked the hook onto the ring on his collar. "Ready to go home?" he asked the dog.

Steve sat in response.

"Remember," Kendall said, "this is a rescue situation. We know he had a prior owner; we think he had a good life before the older man had to give him up. But there's going to be an adjustment period. You have to get to know each other."

"I guess we'll have plenty of time for that, right, Steve?" Julian bent and patted the dog's head. "Kendall, thank you. I'm sure if Steve could talk, he'd say the same thing."

She treated him to a warm, if sad, smile. "Just give him a good life."

"I will," he promised, clenching the leash tighter in his hand.

She met his gaze. "I know."

He fought with himself over what to say next. Whether he should engage her in the conversation *he* needed to have or respect the boundaries she'd erected from the minute he'd walked into the shelter.

She sniffed and brushed a hand beneath her eyes, clearly holding back tears over the dog's departure. Her emotions ran deep, in ways he'd never had the chance to notice before, and his gut clenched, making his decision for him.

"Kendall?"

"Yes?"

Their gazes met and held. "I'm sorry," he said, the words from his heart. "For everything."

Shock flickered in her eyes, followed by a softening, and what he wanted to think was longing settled in her gaze. "Bye, Julian," she whispered.

He inclined his head, accepting that for the dismissal it was. He curled Steve's leash around his hand, winked at her, then turned and walked out of her life.

Chapter Three

JULIAN WAS LOSING his mind. He was surrounded in shit. Literally. Within forty-eight hours of bringing Steve home, the dog got sick... from both ends. He had a vet appointment scheduled at the end of the week for a checkup, and now it was almost five p.m., and of course, Steve was worse. Curled up in a ball on the cool kitchen floor, looking pathetic. He wouldn't eat or drink.

Julian had run the gamut of ideas. He'd sat on the floor and tried to hand-feed. He'd attempted different bowls. Stainless. Ceramic. A damned kitchen plate.

He called the vet he had an appointment with, but the message went straight to voice mail. They'd closed for the day.

Unsure of what else to do, he picked up the phone and dialed the shelter. "Hello, For Paws," Kendall's familiar voice said.

"Kendall, it's Julian."

Silence followed, then, "What can I do for you?"

"Steve's sick." He glanced at the poor dog, looking at him with sad eyes.

"What's wrong?" she asked immediately, concern in her voice. She might not want to speak to him, but she cared about his dog.

Julian drew a deep breath and went on to explain the situation in as delicate a way as he could manage, considering. "The vet I called isn't in and I... I'm at a loss."

She was silent for a few precious seconds. "I'm finished here. I'll come by to check on him. Not that I'm a vet, but we'll figure out what to do. Are you still at the same place?"

"No." He gave her the new address and expelled a breath he hadn't been aware of holding.

Kendall was coming to help him. Kendall. He couldn't even bring himself to process that thought because he had a living, breathing, sick dog on his hands. And he'd never been responsible for anything other than his sister before.

He'd had Steve for two days, and though he should have crated him at night, his cries had been pathetic. So Julian now had a bedmate with bad breath.

He paced the floor, waiting for Kendall to arrive, and finally the bell rang and he opened the door. "Hi. Come on in," he said, relieved to see her.

She wore a similar outfit to the one he'd seen her in the other day, a pair of jeans that molded to her thighs and ass and a tee shirt that said ENJOY THE CRAZY. He appreciated her ability to laugh at life, something she'd been doing since they'd met.

"Where is he?" she asked.

"In the kitchen." He gestured toward the room, and Kendall headed that way. She walked in and discovered Steve lying curled into himself.

"Hey," she crooned to him, getting down on the floor. She put the back of her hand against his nose. "It's warm and dry. There's a twenty-four-hour emergency clinic uptown. Let's take him there."

"Okay, yeah. Good idea." He was relieved someone knew what the hell to do.

She scooped the dog into her arms and rose to her feet "Cab?"

He shook his head. "I can drive."

She met his gaze and nodded. "Okay, let's go."

★ ★ ★

KENDALL HELD ON to a lethargic Steve as Julian sped toward the Upper East Side. She did her best not to look at him, to study his handsome face or masculine features. She didn't want to focus on his full lips or strong jaw. And she especially needed to ignore the woodsy scent in his car. All those things spelled trouble for her deprived senses.

This Julian wasn't the same man as the one she'd

known before. The changes were subtle but they were there. He was more serious, more circumspect. Granted, she'd changed as well, the medication putting her on a more even keel.

She couldn't let herself notice his differences or care.

"Up there. On the right," she said, pointing to the clinic she'd used for Waffles. "There's a parking garage on the corner."

He pulled into the garage and dealt with the attendant. He then walked around to Kendall's side of the car, opening her door before she could maneuver with Steve.

"He's heavy. Let me carry him up the street."

She reluctantly handed the dog over. They made their way up the street and entered the clinic. Kendall took over holding Steve while Julian filled out paperwork. Luckily the clinic wasn't busy, and they were quickly ushered into the examining room.

The vet, a doctor Kendall had met before, walked in to greet them. Dr. Drake did a quick, thorough exam, making Steve suffer through the indignity of having his temperature taken, his gums looked at, and his heart listened to, among other things.

The doctor ran through a list of questions with Julian. Steve hadn't gotten into food or anything else he shouldn't have, the only change being the food Julian had picked up for the dog at the store.

"Okay, it looks like he's got an upset stomach. Whether it's from the change in living arrangement because he's sensitive or the new food, I don't know. I'd like to give him fluids under his skin to prevent dehydration from the vomiting and diarrhea. There'll be a lump in his back for one to two days while the fluids disperse through his body, but it's nothing to be concerned about," the doctor explained.

Julian watched the doctor intently, listening to every word. The vet went on to discuss the medicines he'd send him home with.

Although the vet and tech worked together, holding Steve, Julian stood in front of the dog, reassuring him, whispering to him, and smoothing a hand over his head while they inserted the needle and fluid.

Kendall's heart squeezed hard inside her chest, emotion flowing through her. Unwanted emotion. Softening feelings for a man who'd all but destroyed her.

No, no, no!

"Kendall, did you say something?" Julian asked.

"No." God, had she spoken out loud?

The vet pulled the plastic gloves off his hands. "Okay, you were a good boy," he said to Steve. "Now, as for food. As he starts to feel better, you can either give him ground beef and rice or I can send you home with canned food that will be bland on his stomach."

"Canned," both Kendall and Julian said at the same time, because she couldn't see Julian cooking for the dog. From what she remembered, he didn't cook much for himself, either.

He glanced her way and grinned. "Mind meld," he said, chuckling.

He used to say that when they'd be on the same wavelength, when they were seeing each other before. She hadn't been surprised the tech geek was a *Star Trek* fan. She wasn't comfortable their thoughts were syncing now.

The vet finished up with Steve, and once again, Kendall held him, this time while Julian paid the bill. Soon they were on their way back to his apartment, enclosed in his delicious-smelling car.

"Thank you for coming when I called," he said, pulling out of the parking garage and into traffic on the city roads.

"You're welcome. I was worried about Steve," she said, petting his soft head. He lay quietly in her lap.

She glanced over in time to catch his smirk.

"I didn't think you did it for me," he said.

She blew out a short breath. "Julian, I don't think now is the time—"

"You're a captive audience here in my car, kitten. There's no better time."

A full-body shiver took hold at the nickname. Her temperature heated, her nipples puckered, and if she hadn't already been aware of him from his scent and sweet behavior with Steve, she was now.

She remained silent. He had something to say, and she was going to have to listen.

"When I met you, I was a fucked up mess," he said, taking her off guard. "We never talked about it, but I'm an addict," he said, his grip on the steering wheel so hard his knuckles turned white.

"My sister told me," she said softly. Because suddenly this conversation was serious, and if he was going to be so honest, he didn't need her snark.

"I was clean when we got together, not that I'd use it as an excuse if I wasn't. That's what I want to tell you. There is no excuse for what I did to you."

She blinked, her eyes suddenly watery.

"I mean, I had reasons for my behavior that I used to justify what I did at the time, and they aren't important now. Because they'd only come off sounding like what they are. Bullshit excuses for poor behavior. Whatever was between me and Kade should have stayed between us. I shouldn't have dragged you into it. And while I'm at it, I shouldn't have gone after him in that kind of underhanded way, either," he said, jaw clenched, the words obviously difficult for him to say.

She knew her mouth was hanging open, and she

managed to close it before he turned to glance at her. An apology was one thing. A flat-out *I was an asshole* was quite another. She hadn't expected such brutal sincerity.

She swallowed over the lump in her throat. "Pull over."

"What?"

"Pull over. I can't have this conversation while you're driving." If not for the fact that her hands were on Steve's body, she'd be shaking. The discussion was way deeper than she'd anticipated.

Julian did as she asked, gliding into the first available parking spot on the street. He put the car in park and turned to face her.

Her mouth grew dry. "I'm not sure what to say. I didn't expect you to be that honest and apologetic."

His face turned red, and he ran a hand through his hair. "Fact is, for a long time it was hard for me to look at myself in the mirror."

She continued to pet Steve. "Why is now different? What changed?"

Silence descended and she squirmed in her seat, waiting.

"I found out about you." He stretched an arm across the back of her seat. "I didn't know you were bipolar, and finding out forced me to face myself."

"You mean it was okay to do it to a woman who

was mentally stable?" she asked, horrified.

He shook his head. "Of course not. It's just that I'd convinced myself you could handle it, and I discovered I had you at an even bigger disadvantage than not knowing I had an agenda." He shook his head. "This is coming out all wrong."

She ran a shaking hand through her hair. "You didn't devastate me because I had an illness, Julian. You hurt me because I was falling for you, and every word, every action, was a lie."

"That's what changed." He let his fingertips trail over her shoulder.

She knew she should pull back, but just that small touch bridging the gap between them felt so good.

"The pretense of us being strangers, that was a lie. The growing feelings went both ways. And when I realized how badly I hurt you, how little I knew you, I realized I was devastated, too."

Shock rippled through her body along with a healthy dose of disbelief. "You really expect me to believe you?" she asked, but a part of her did. And that frightened her.

"No." He slid his hand behind her neck and pulled her close so her forehead touched his. "But I want the chance to convince you."

★ ★ ★

JULIAN DIDN'T KNOW where the words came from. He hadn't planned to ask Kendall for anything, but he meant them with every fiber of his being. He wanted a second chance, something he had no right to request any more than he had the right to kiss her.

But he did, capturing her mouth with his. She jolted in surprise but immediately relaxed into him. Heart pounding, he took in every nuance, her soft, warm lips, lingering familiar scent, and unique taste that electrified his body. But he held back, being deliberately gentle, so unlike their frenetic couplings in the past, but that special connection hadn't changed.

He licked her lower lip, and she leaned in closer, ignoring the squirming dog. He slid his tongue over hers, causing sparks to fly between them. He tasted her, devoured her, but it wasn't enough. He wrapped his hand around her ponytail and tugged, tilting her head, giving him better access to the deep recesses of her mouth.

Kissing her was like coming home, like everything bad in his life hadn't happened, and he lost himself in the moment. Until a bark disrupted them and brought her back to reality.

She jerked back, startled, petting Steve's head. "I don't even know what to say, but that shouldn't have happened." Her hands shook as she trailed them over the dog's back. "I'll get a cab from here." She pulled at the handle of the door, seeking to get out, but it was locked.

"Let me drive you home." He didn't want her stranded here, even though they were in a perfectly good neighborhood.

"You need to let me go, Julian."

He swallowed hard, and, respecting her wishes, he hit the unlock button. She yanked open the door, climbed out, and put Steve gently on the passenger seat. She touched him one last time before meeting Julian's gaze. "Bye," she whispered. She straightened and slammed the door shut.

He closed his eyes, smarting from her words. They hurt. But he didn't blame her for being scared. He did, however, know what existed between them, what that kiss had reignited.

He watched as she hailed a cab, waiting until she was safely inside one before pulling back onto the street.

He glanced at Steve, who met his gaze and yawned. "Yeah, I know. I didn't want her to leave, either." But after that kiss, he had hope. She'd run, but she would think. And that's all he could ask for.

★ ★ ★

As soon as Kendall got home, she took Waffles for a long walk. Not only did her dog need the exercise, she needed to think, and she had to do it alone.

Kendall couldn't tell her sister about seeing Julian. Lexie wouldn't understand. She was protective of Kendall, for good reason. Even if Kendall felt she could now make her own positive decisions, no matter what they might be, her twin needed time to learn the same thing.

This was when Kendall found life the hardest. Not having a close friend to go to and discuss girl things—because Lexie was her person. And Kendall, during her many mood phases, had driven everyone else away. She was just starting to rebuild her life with people like Josie. One step, one person at a time.

She swallowed hard. She would have to work through her feelings both on her own and with her therapist. And boy, did she have feelings. That kiss had ignited a firestorm of emotions inside her. Ones she'd thought she'd buried when she stopped letting herself think about Julian.

He'd been so gentle, so tender. So unlike the man he'd been when they were together before. Oh, the chemistry was just as potent now, but there was an emotional element that was fresh and new. Kendall hadn't been capable of digging that deep into herself then. She was now, and she sensed all of the emotion Julian had poured into that one kiss. There was a caring she couldn't deny. No matter how much her rational self wanted to. Watching him with Steve, the sweetness he'd shown the dog had affected her, too.

And his apology. *I'm sorry* was easy to say. Meaning it was something else entirely, and he'd obviously given his behavior real thought. He seemed to own his mistakes.

But hadn't she believed him before?

He'd swept into her life like a storm, flirting with her at the gym, complimenting her, finding all they had in common, and yeah, sweeping her off her feet. Of course, she'd been on a high at the time, all too amenable to his charms.

She paused when Waffles stopped to do his business, cleaning up after him and tossing the bag into the nearest trash before heading back home.

Julian wanted a second chance, and damn him, he'd begun making inroads, chipping away at her hurt and anger. She knew what it was like to make mistakes, to need someone else to see beyond the past and accept her apology. How could she offer him anything less than what she'd received herself? From Lexie. From Kade.

But along with that acceptance came the belief that maybe he really had changed. And if so, if he was a different man, then she couldn't help but wonder if things between them could be different this time. Because the hard truth was she hadn't stopped wanting him. Their searing kiss had proven that. But beyond the physical yearning to be close to him was an emotional pull, too.

Waffles rushed ahead, and she tugged on the leash, slowing him down. She wasn't quite ready to let Julian go for good, and that scared her because she didn't know if she could trust her instincts… or him.

★　★　★

THE NEXT DAY, Kendall was dragging from lack of sleep. She knew she had thoughts of Julian to blame, but she pushed herself to perk up and show up at work on time. She let herself inside, a Starbucks coffee in either hand.

"You look exhausted," Josie said as soon as Kendall walked in the door.

"I'm beat. But there's caffeine to help make it easier. I brought you a cup." She placed the grande on the desk where Josie sat.

"Thank you. I think I love you," she said, taking a long sip.

Kendall laughed. "I wasn't going to make it without some." She lived on vanilla chais. She tossed her bag onto her desk and settled into her chair.

"Sorry I had to leave early yesterday. What did I miss?" Josie asked.

Only everything, Kendall thought wryly. "Julian

had a problem with Steve last night." She went on to explain how she'd gone to his place and accompanied him to the vet. "I know it's not standard protocol for us to join them for a vet visit after adoption, but he sounded so distraught."

"And it was Steve. And you're invested. I know," Josie said, meeting her gaze. "Is he okay?"

Kendall nodded. "He was dehydrated. They gave him sub-q fluids and a bland diet and medicine. I don't know how he was overnight or this morning." She was curious, but she hesitated to call and renew contact.

"I can check in… unless you want to do it?" Josie asked. "I mean, you did step up last night and help. And didn't you say you two knew each other?"

Kendall wanted to confide in Josie, but how much did she tell her? They were friends, but they weren't so close that she knew about Kendall's past. She'd been hesitant to give her the full rundown, not wanting to lose her job because she'd provided reasons for her boss to distrust her. Or not want to be her friend. Kendall had reason to be cautious.

"We have history," she admitted about Julian.

"Romantic history?" Josie asked, a grin on her face. "Because that was some thick tension between you two the other day."

"Mmm hmm."

Josie rolled her eyes, at the same time treating her

to a knowing grin. "And that's all I'm going to get, obviously."

"It's really complicated, and I have to decide what to do about it." And that, Kendall thought, was an understatement.

"Would it help if I did the check-in?"

Kendall shook her head, knowing this was something she needed to do herself. "No. Thanks. I can handle it." And him.

She hoped.

"Okay, I'm off to check out the kennels, then. Man the fort up here."

"Will do." Kendall waited until Josie walked out before picking up her cell and calling Julian.

He answered on the first ring. "Hey there," he said, sounding happy to hear from her, his voice, deep and rumbly this morning, causing a shiver to ripple over her skin.

"Morning. How was Steve last night?" she asked before he could wonder about her reasons for calling.

"I couldn't take the whining. He sounded so damned pathetic, so I scooped him up and put him in my bed. Again. Slept like a baby all night."

Lucky dog. She bit her tongue to keep the words from spilling out.

"And this morning, he ate up the canned food, which smells like shit, by the way, and he seems more like himself. Except for the lump on his back from the water. Makes him look like the Hunchback of Notre Dame. Other than that, all's well here."

She exhaled a relieved breath. "I'm glad to hear it." Now, she needed to hang up. Get off the phone before—

"So I was thinking," he went on, oblivious to her thoughts. "I feel bad for Steve. He's in a new place and has no friends."

She shook her head and laughed, an unwilling smile lifting the corners of her mouth. "He has you. I'm sure he'll survive."

"Well, I don't know about that. The poor guy's coming from a shelter with lots of dogs, you know? So I was thinking, what if we introduced him to your dog?"

"Wait. What?"

"Waffles. Isn't that her name?"

"Yes, but—"

"Every guy needs a good girl in his life."

God, now he was being cute and sweet. "Julian—"

"Not to mention, I need to find a good dog park, and I'm sure you take Waffles to one, right?"

"Yes. Near my apartment." She gripped the phone tighter in her hand.

"So what if we met up there this weekend?"

Her head was spinning at the speed of this conversation. She wondered if he was doing it on purpose, keeping her off-balance so she wouldn't hang up the phone or dismiss him out of hand.

"You want to meet at the dog park. This weekend."

"I figure Steve will be one hundred percent well by then."

She swallowed hard. This wasn't about the dogs, not entirely. She knew that, but in making the invitation more about their pets, he was taking the pressure off. One friend showing another friend, a new dog owner, the ropes. Yes, that was her story and she was sticking to it.

She could meet him at the dog park during a busy time, and they wouldn't be alone. It would be low-key.

"Kendall, are you still there?" he asked.

She shook her head, forcing herself to focus on the conversation and not the thoughts circling around in her head. "Okay, if it's good weather, I could do it on Saturday," she heard herself saying before she'd actually decided it was safe for her to see him again. She'd also have a therapy appointment in between to shore up her defenses.

"Great! Text me the address and the time that works, and I'll meet you there. Steve said to say thanks. He's in the market for a girlfriend," he said, laughing.

She couldn't help but smile. This, too, was a new side to Julian. Easy, carefree, not intense. "Sounds good," she murmured.

"It's a date," he said, and before she could correct him, he said good-bye and disconnected the call.

Chapter Four

KENDALL WAS INVITED to dinner with Lexie, Kade, and his business partner, Derek West, and his wife, Cassie. Even Lucas Monroe and his wife, Maxie, were here, Lucas's parents at home with the couple's new baby girl, Sarah.

The fact that Lucas's parents had accepted him and Maxie as a couple was big news, as Maxie had once been married to Lucas's asshole brother, who'd manipulated them to keep the couple apart since they were young. Kendall took heart from their success and hoped her family would someday be as generous—if things with Julian went further.

The restaurant was an upscale French bistro with a Parisian feel, bold flowers peeking out of the corners, the atmosphere quiet and surprisingly welcoming.

She knew it had taken the pull of the billionaires to get them a table, and she looked forward to trying a new place. She looked forward to tasting the three-Michelin-star food prepared by the world-renowned chef, the highest amount of stars given. Even if she wasn't sure what to choose and decided to copy what her sister ordered, just to be safe.

Kendall wore a burgundy fitted dress with bone pumps, while Lexie chose a navy dress, Maxie a winter-white one, and Cassie a pretty floral. The men wore suits, which was unusual for them as they did enjoy their denim, Kendall thought wryly. Like Julian, none of the guys came from super wealthy backgrounds. Everyone was self-made, and they remained true to who they were to begin with.

Derek ordered wine and even Kade gave up his usual Macallen scotch that he drank in a very... Kade-like way, to join everyone with a glass of wine. The waiter poured, and Derek tested, red, and now they had their glasses full.

Kendall could take a sip or two if she wanted, but she didn't love wine enough to bother, and Maxie was breastfeeding, so she'd bypassed the alcohol, too.

They placed their orders, and they could finally talk to each other without being interrupted by a waiter with specials, requesting drink orders, or taking their dinner choices.

"How are things going at Storms Consolidated?" Lexie asked Cassie, who had taken over her family media business when, after a lot of complications, angst, and drama, Derek bought the company and put her in charge.

Derek laced his fingers through hers and placed

their joined hands on top of the table. "She's making major changes."

Kendall knew that Cassie had wanted to bring the company into the modern world, something her father had failed at doing, and focus more on online subscribers and technology.

"And the article she wrote about me, much as I hated being the center of attention, really turned things around for Take a Byte," he said of the online magazine Cassie ran. "Advertisers are impressed, and she has other subjects booked for upcoming months," he added with obvious pride.

"You're too sweet," Cassie murmured, her gaze lovingly on Derek. "I'm trying hard to make it work," she said to the rest of the table.

He kissed the back of her hand, the moment suddenly intimate. But when Kendall looked at her sister, Kade was gazing at her the same way. And Lucas and Maxie were busy both looking at her cell phone.

Kendall shifted uncomfortably in her seat, feeling like the odd man out in a mix of loving couples. She knew they weren't trying to make her uncomfortable on purpose. They were all good people who had supported her when they could have turned their backs, who'd taken her in as a friend, and who she genuinely liked.

Yet as she looked around, she'd never felt more

alone.

It wasn't their fault. Each person was a part of a couple. She wasn't. They were friends through their significant others. Kendall came to them through her sister. For a while, that had been enough, but now she needed more of her own life and plans.

Like Julian? the devil on her shoulder asked.

"So, Kendall, are you seeing anyone?" Cassie asked hopefully, breaking into her traitorous, unwanted thoughts.

The women were always suggesting different men for her to date in an attempt to be helpful. Kendall appreciated the effort but had wanted to move forward on her own time. When she knew she was over Julian completely and ready to try again.

Now he was back. And she couldn't tell anyone at this table. Not even about something as innocent as a trip to the dog park. Because Julian had, in one way or another, stabbed all of these men in the back.

Kendall pasted a happy smile on her face. "No, nobody new," she said.

"Well, we just hired this new reporter and he's hot." Cassie fanned her hand in front of her face.

"Oh, Kendall? What do you think? Are you up for a blind date?" Lexie asked, nudging her with her arm.

"You have to get back in the saddle sometime," Kade said, ever-not-so-helpfully.

Typical man.

"Not right now," Kendall said. "But I'll be sure to let you know when I'm ready."

"Okay," Maxie said, sounding disappointed.

"Is it good to get way from the little one?" Derek asked Maxie and Lucas, changing the subject. "Or are you dying to get home?"

"She's only checked her phone every two seconds for a text from my mother," Lucas said lovingly.

"Like you're any different? You keep asking me if I've heard anything!" Maxie said with a laugh.

And from there, they were on to conversation about babies. Kendall shifted in her seat.

As far as she was concerned, tomorrow couldn't get here fast enough, something the people at this table would be horrified to find out about.

★　★　★

KENDALL OVERDRESSED FOR the dog park, all the while annoyed with herself for caring what she looked like to meet Julian. But the last two times she'd seen him, she'd been at her grungy worst, and pride demanded she pull herself together today and make a good impression.

She sifted through her closet, changing more than once. Ultimately she chose a pair of tight jeans that accentuated her curves, a light pink top with open shoulders, and a pair of black slip-on ballet flats. She brushed her hair, keeping it down and flowing over her shoulders, and dusted on a light amount of makeup.

She and her therapist had talked in preparation for today's *date*. True to form, the doctor hadn't offered an opinion either way on what to do about Julian and his reappearance in her life. She had, however, thrown questions at Kendall for her to think about. Things like, did she trust her instincts lately? Yes, yes she did. More and more, in fact.

Did she think people could change? A loaded question, since Kendall obviously knew *she* had. But she was on medication, she'd reminded her doctor. But all that did was stabilize what was already inside Kendall.

What did Kendall think was inside Julian? A good man? A bad one? And did she want to find out?

By the time her appointment had ended, all Kendall knew was that she had a dog date with Julian, which would provide time for Kendall to watch him, get to know him again, and lean on her instincts.

No time like the present, she thought, glancing at her prancing dog, who knew from the leash in her hand they were going out.

"You ready to make a friend?" she asked Waffles, holding out her harness.

The dog began to circle around, and Kendall hooked her up, clasped the leash, grabbed her messenger bag, put on her sunglasses, and was ready to go.

She headed out, more excited for this morning than she'd been for her dinner last night.

She still felt guilty for not mentioning today's plans to her sister. She didn't like lying, even by omission, but there was no way she could have explained the situation to anyone at the table.

Besides, it was just one friend doing another friend a favor, showing him where to hang out with his dog.

Liar.

She frowned at her inner voice. Because the fact remained that Julian wanted more from Kendall than friendship—and a part of Kendall desired more, too. Something she'd have to take one step at a time, if at all.

There was so much they didn't know about each other. So many things that had changed about her since they'd been together last.

She glanced up as she walked. White clouds dotted the sky, and the temperature was in the mid-seventies. In the sun, she didn't need a jacket, but she'd tied a sweatshirt around her waist, just in case.

Nerves dancing in her stomach, she arrived at the park early and settled in to wait, releasing Waffles into the gated area so she could play. On such a beautiful day, the park was crowded with different dogs and their owners, and Kendall recognized a few people from her prior trips here. She said hello and waited for Julian.

Right on time, he arrived, gorgeous as ever in a pair of dark jeans and a white tee shirt, his biceps flexing, arm tattoo visible, giving him a sexy air. Add to that the aviators on his eyes and his dark hair glinting in the sun, and he simply took her breath away.

In one hand, he carried a cardboard tray with two Starbucks cups in the holders. Steve trotted along beside him, gray ears flopping as he walked. He looked happy and a lot healthier than the last time she'd seen him, and she smiled in relief.

"Hey, little man!" Kendall said to Steve, waiting until Julian let himself inside the gate and closed it behind him before she knelt down to greet the dog. "You look so much better." She petted his soft head before rising to her feet and meeting Julian's amused stare.

"I hope you're as happy to see me." He winked, causing her stomach to pitch and pleasure and arousal to flood through her, her breasts suddenly full, her nipples hard and visible beneath her shirt.

"I'm pleased to see you both," she admitted.

"I brought drinks. A grande vanilla chai for you."

"You remembered," she said, touched by the gesture.

He smiled. "When it comes to you, I couldn't forget."

Unnerved, she focused on pulling the cup from the holder and removing his as well. He tossed the cardboard in the nearest trash can, released Steve from his leash, and let him join in the dog fun.

"Here." She handed him his coffee.

"So this is where the cool dog parents hang out, hmm?"

She laughed, looking over the dogs playing, wrestling, tussling for dominance. "It's a nice-sized area and it's clean. The people who come here are pretty respectful with their dogs. Oh, look!" She gestured to where Steve and Waffles had found one another.

Waffles nudged Steve with her nose, then assumed a stiff pose, waiting for some kind of reaction. Steve, on the other hand, shifted his body and froze in another position, each waiting to see what the other would do. Eventually they were rolling around on the ground, wrestling like old friends.

"Steve's got good taste," Julian said, folding his arms across his chest as he watched his dog play. "I guess it runs in the family."

Her cheeks warmed, and it wasn't from the heat of the sun. "Julian," she said in a warning tone. She wasn't ready to have an intimate conversation with him about feelings.

"So let's catch up," he said. As if sensing her discomfort, he quickly changed the subject. "How did you end up working at the shelter?"

She blew out a breath, relaxing at the easy, softball question. She immediately decided if he wanted to have any kind of relationship with her, he needed to know everything—and choose whether to be her friend or to run far and fast.

"Well," she said, wrapping her hands around the warm cup, "when I got out of the hospital and Lexie gave Waffles back to me, I knew I needed to start life fresh and get a job."

"Whoa. Wait. Hospital? When were you in the hospital?"

She ran her tongue over her dry lips. The bench had opened up, and she gestured toward it. "Let's sit."

They settled in, and she turned toward him, her knees touching his. "You know I'm bipolar, and after what happened with you and what I did, stealing Kade's watch, pawning it... I knew I needed more help than weekly therapy could give."

He dipped his chin and glanced away. "You did those things because I encouraged you to."

She shook her head. "I did those things because it gave me a rush. A high. I was sick, and to be honest, yes, you played into my illness." She put the coffee cup down and twisted her hands together.

He covered her hands in his, and she appreciated the comfort he tried to give. "You don't need to do this."

"Yes. I do. Because I think you have this skewed version of who I am in your head. Once you know the truth, you'll run far and fast, like everyone else," she muttered before drawing a deep breath and continuing.

"Anyway, I spent my life letting my sister clean up my messes and take care of me, and I treated her so badly. So after I found out the truth—that you set me up, knew who I was, used me to get to Kade... and I allowed it—I knew something had to change. So I checked myself into Maple Hill, an inpatient psychiatric facility."

He placed a warm hand on the back of her neck. "Relax," he murmured. "And breathe."

Her entire body was rigid, she realized, her gaze focused on the playing dogs, because she'd been waiting for his shock, then horror, then any excuse to get away from the *mental patient*.

She pulled in a ragged breath and exhaled, forcing herself to take in much-needed air and allowing her muscles to ease up.

"I didn't know about the hospital, but it doesn't

change what I think of you. Now go on. I believe I asked you how you got the job at the shelter."

He wasn't running. He still wanted to get to know her. Relief rushed through her as that truth settled in. "Right. The shelter. When I got out of the hospital, medicated and more in control of myself, I needed a job. I'd bought Waffles during one of my manic phases, but she gave me focus in those early days. And I realized that's what I was good at. Dealing with animals. I started walking the neighbors' dogs, turned that into a business, and found the shelter job, too."

"You found your calling." His hand remained on the back of her neck, his thumb gently rubbing back and forth. What started as comfort was fast turning to sexual awareness.

It had never taken much with Julian in the past. A look. A kiss. And they'd duck into the nearest coat closet in a hotel, lock a single-person restroom and go at it there. The doctors explained her heightened sexual need was part of her illness, but she had to admit, she wanted him still.

She tilted her head and met his gaze. "I guess I'm the female dog whisperer." She grinned.

"You're certainly my whisperer," he said in a husky voice, his face close to hers.

His mossy-green eyes grew darker, and she thought he was going to kiss her. Her body was primed and ready, her heart beating inside her chest, her sex damp. Just from the thought of a public kiss.

She pulled in a deep breath, and he moved in, sliding his nose along the side of hers. "Nothing you said changed my mind," he whispered. "I want a second chance."

It wasn't a claiming of her mouth; it was so much more. But she had reservations. "I don't know. There's so much … pain between us."

But the man in front of her wasn't the same guy she'd known. She felt it deep in her gut.

"How about we just get to know each other again? No pressure."

"What did you have in mind?" she asked.

"Well, tomorrow night I'm going for dinner at a very good friend's house. You spoke to him on the phone. Nick Cantone. He's also my AA sponsor. An alcoholic." He paused a beat, letting that piece of information sink in before going on.

"I have dinner with his family on Sunday nights, and I'd like it very much if you came with me. Getting to know them will help you get to know me."

In his expression, she saw a vulnerability that was new. A fear she would reject him. He hadn't run at her big revelation. She wasn't about to run at his.

AA. Alcoholics Anonymous. He'd mentioned that once before, in the car when he'd apologized. He, too, was working on his issues. She didn't have to think twice about her answer.

"I'd love to come." She didn't know what she was getting herself into, but she couldn't deny she wanted to find out.

The rest of the afternoon didn't involve anything serious in the way of conversation. Instead they talked about his job, the building of his business, and the surprises involved with adopting a pet.

He picked up a stick and threw it. Steve ran for the object and brought it back to Julian. "Good boy!" He petted the dog on his head. "All that ball tossing in the apartment paid off." He glanced at Kendall. "I throw toward the bathroom. He's got room to run and retrieve."

"I'm impressed." She picked up a different stick and tried the same thing with Waffles.

The fluffy dog ran, picked up the stick, lay down, and began chewing on it.

"Terriers," Kendall muttered. "They have a stubborn mind of their own."

Julian laughed. "She definitely does her own thing." He met her gaze, laughter in the green depths. "This has been fun," he said. "We should do it again."

Pleasure suffused her at his suggestion. "Because the dogs are now best friends?" She gestured to where the two pets were now tussling for the same stick.

"That's one reason. And because, like I said, I want us to be more."

★ ★ ★

JULIAN HEADED TO pick up Kendall for his dinner at the Cantones'. Every time he recalled her agreeing to join him, he released a breath and sat up straighter, knowing he'd accomplished something important during their trip to the dog park. He'd gotten her back into his life.

Baby steps, he thought, the whole experience putting him on edge. What did he know about taking it slow? Baring his soul? But he was doing it, wasn't he? She was joining him for what would be as close to a family dinner as he could have.

He'd never known his father, who'd abandoned the family when Julian was nine and his sister, Alyssa, was one. They hadn't gotten along anyway, except clearly they'd gotten together, because Alyssa was an oops baby, as his mother liked to say. His mother had turned into a functioning alcoholic, as Julian thought of her. She'd worked and raised her children, but alcohol was her crutch and always in her system.

Julian had sworn he'd never let a substance dictate how he lived or behaved. Damned ironic. That was exactly what he'd done. His mother's trigger had been his father's leaving. Julian's trigger had been his sister's

71

accident. Not something he liked to think about, but he'd dealt with it enough, so for now he pushed that thought away and focused on the night ahead.

He'd never brought a woman to meet his friends, let alone *this* friend, his sponsor and the man who'd all but saved his life. And knew him best.

Kendall opened the door, wearing a V-neck, multi-color draped dress in light blue tones. Her eyes sparkled, her cheeks were bright, and he caught a glimpse of the woman he'd known, who was always up for any adventure.

"Looking good, kitten," he said, wrapping an arm around her waist and kissing her on the cheek. He wanted to do more, but "tread lightly" was his motto.

She blushed. "Thank you." She turned to Waffles, who was nuzzling her head against Julian's jean-clad legs. "Be good, girl. I'll be back later," Kendall said.

Waffles whined in response.

"We'll bring you to see Steve again soon," Julian promised in an attempt to soothe the dog.

She whined again and lay down on the floor, gazing up at him with pathetic eyes.

"Are they born knowing how to make us guilty? Steve does the same thing."

Kendall laughed, the sound light and airy, going right to his groin.

"Ignore her. She's perfected the sad face. I have a camera here and an app on my phone. I can see her while I'm gone. She sleeps the whole time. Bye, puppy." She blew a kiss, grabbed a bakery box from the counter, and they walked out the door.

She led him to the elevator, giving him a view of her spectacularly tight ass, hips swaying as she walked ahead of him.

Nick and his wife, Lauren, lived in a two-bedroom on the Upper West Side. The apartment was for sale because they were ready to move to a house in the suburbs, but they hadn't been able to sell it for what they wanted yet. Julian would miss them living in the city and attending the same meetings, but like everything else in life, he'd adjust. He was just grateful he was finally in a good place and didn't have to rely on Nick as he had in the past.

Together he and Kendall took a cab to their destination, the driver talking to them the entire way. Kendall shot him an amused smile, and impulse had him reaching out and grabbing her hand and running his thumb over her soft skin.

Her eyes opened wide, but she didn't pull away, which gave him a silent thrill as they sped through Manhattan.

Chapter Five

KENDALL TREMBLED FROM the way Julian looked at her from the minute she'd opened the door. He had a way of making her feel beautiful with just that sexy glint in his eye, and she had to admit, a girl could get used to feeling that way. They were also growing more comfortable around each other, something else she couldn't help but notice. And it was only the second time she'd seen him... or this new and improved version of him, anyway.

Once they arrived at the Cantones' apartment, Kendall didn't have time to be nervous. They were greeted by Nick, a good-looking man who appeared slightly older than Julian, with gray streaks in his hair, and his wife, a bubbly, petite blonde named Lauren, and their ten-year-old son, Brian.

"Uncle Julian!" The boy, with light brown hair, barreled into Julian in his excitement to see him.

"Hey!" Julian did some kind of weird guy-bonding handshake with the little boy.

Kendall's heart did an unfamiliar thump at the sight of the man and the child together. It was an adorable sight to see.

"I'm so happy to meet you," Lauren said, interrupting her thoughts as she grasped Kendall's hand.

"Thank you for inviting me." She held out the box of bakery cookies she'd bought to bring with her.

"You didn't have to, but thanks! Come, join me in the kitchen. I just have to put the finishing touches on dinner."

Julian met her gaze, and she reassured him with a nod and a smile. She could handle herself, and Lauren seemed friendly.

They left the men alone and headed for the kitchen, which was a simple setup, white walls and stainless steel appliances. City apartments were so small; it was obvious why the couple was ready to move out.

"Can I get you something to drink? I'd offer you wine, but I don't keep alcohol in the house." She glanced at Kendall, a knowing look in her gaze.

Kendall understood Lauren's husband was a recovering alcoholic and nodded in reply. "A Diet Coke would be great. I don't drink, either." She drew a deep breath, deciding on honesty from the start. "Bipolar meds don't mix well with alcohol," she said.

There was every chance Julian had already told Lauren and Nick all about her, and this was his family. She didn't mind sharing.

Lauren treated her to a warm smile. "We all deal

with something, don't we?" She opened the oven and put on protective mitts, pulling out a lasagna. "So Julian's never brought a woman around before. This is a big deal." She placed the casserole tin on the cooling tray on the preset kitchen table. "*You're* a big deal."

Kendall felt her cheeks heat. "I don't know about that. Julian and I have a complicated history. I think, by bringing me here, he wants me to see him in a different light."

"And do you?" Lauren asked.

Kendall froze. She wasn't ready to discuss her feelings for Julian with a stranger, even one as friendly as Lauren. She'd barely pieced them together herself.

The other woman shook her head. "I'm sorry. That's none of my business. I have a habit of being too forward. Just ask my husband. I invited him on our first date."

She laughed at herself, and Kendall liked her even more.

"Let's talk about something else," Lauren suggested. "Julian tells me you work at a dog shelter." She picked up the pitcher of water and placed it on the table.

"The shelter is in Midtown." And Kendall loved talking about her work. "There's no better feeling than to place dogs that come in desperately needing homes."

Lauren spun back around. "Wonderful! Because when we move out of the city, soon I hope, I promised Brian a dog. I should come check out your shelter."

"Any time. We have an open door, and sadly, we get new dogs all the time."

"You can leave the information over there." Lauren pointed to a notepad and pen by the phone.

Kendall did as she asked, then turned back. "Is there anything I can do to help?"

"Actually I'm all set. Boys!" Lauren called out, her voice rising. "Dinner's ready!"

A few seconds later, the two men and the little boy walked into the room, continuing their conversation as they took their seats. Julian pulled out a chair next to Kendall, while Brian grabbed the next closest one to Julian. The little boy had a cute case of hero worship going on for his *Uncle Julian*.

The food was delicious; the talk around the table was easy and comfortable. Brian was thrilled to discover Kendall walked dogs and had a ton of questions on the different breeds. She, of course, taught him the benefits of rescue. He was adorable and sweet, and she couldn't wait to help match him with the right pet.

"So, Kendall, where did you and Julian meet?" Lauren asked as they were finishing up.

Beneath the table, Julian slid a hand onto her thigh, as if sensing she'd be treading on a sensitive subject. Obviously Lauren didn't know minute details of their past, so Kendall pushed away the painful part of the memories, that Julian had targeted her, and focused on the day she'd first seen him and the feelings he'd inspired instead.

"We met at the gym," she said, unable not to smile at the recollection. "He approached me as I was stepping off the treadmill and asked if I wanted to get coffee sometime." It had seemed so genuine, so innocent in the moment.

After all, if a guy wanted to go out with you after seeing you at your sweaty worst, he was interested. Or so she'd thought. She swallowed hard. Focusing on his mistakes would be a surefire way to destroy any progress they'd made.

Julian's hand squeezed tighter on her thigh, and though he meant to comfort, her body reacted in a purely sexual way. A ripple of desire shot through her, and a sweet pulsing settled in her sex, traveling outward, to the tightened peaks of her nipples.

"Kendall? Are you okay? Lauren asked.

"I'm fine," she managed to say. She took a sip of water in an attempt to cool her body down.

The one place she and Julian had always clicked was in bed. Kendall, during a manic episode, craved sex… probably the way an addict like Julian once craved drugs. And he'd been all too happy to provide her fix.

On the wrong meds, she'd been reckless. She hadn't worried about being caught. And those memories swamped her now.

"Julian, how's your sister doing?" Lauren's voice brought Kendall back to the present. "Is the flower shop job working out for her?"

"Sister?" Kendall asked. She didn't know he had a sibling. He'd never mentioned it.

Another nod to how caught up she'd been in their sexual desire… and he'd probably been focused on getting her to do his bidding when it came to her brother-in-law. They hadn't taken the time to really get to know the important things about each other.

"Yes. My sister's name is Alyssa. She's eight years younger than me."

Another squeeze of her thigh; this one she took as a promise to explain more later. She hoped.

Julian cleared his throat. "She's doing well," he said to Lauren, his voice raspier than usual. "The routine of the job is good for her condition."

Kendall narrowed her gaze. Something more was at play here, but she didn't feel it was the right time to ask.

"That's great," Nick said.

"She sends her love to everyone and said she hopes to see you all soon."

"Can I be 'scused?" Brian asked. "I want to watch TV."

"Sure," Lauren said. "Go wash up and I'll come check on you in a little while."

He ran out of the room and Nick shook his head. "I can't wait until we can send him out back to expend some of that energy in a yard."

"I don't blame you," Julian said.

"Lauren, can I help you clean up?" Kendall started to rise, but Lauren shook her head.

"No, please. You're my guest."

"No. I insist."

The other woman smiled. "And I'd do the same thing. Fine. You can help me clear the table, but that's it. Boys, go talk. We'll be out in a few minutes."

"I think I can manage to move my plate across the room," Julian said.

They worked together, and soon enough, the sink was full and Lauren insisted she'd clean later.

After another half hour of talk in the living room, Julian rose. "It's time for us to get going."

Good-byes were said, Lauren promising to come visit her at the shelter, and soon they were out on the street.

"My apartment isn't far from here. Want to head

there and talk?" Julian asked. "I'm sure you have questions about Alyssa."

His previously unmentioned sister. "I do," Kendall said, but she wasn't sure being alone with him at his place was the right thing to do.

She looked in his serious green eyes and found herself nodding. Because when had she ever been smart when it came to Julian Dane?

★ ★ ★

JULIAN NOW LIVED in a nicer building on the West Side, his apartment in a better area courtesy of his settlement with Blink. Although there were many things he felt guilty about, the settlement money ultimately wasn't one of them because he had been in on the ground floor of creating the app. Many of the core elements had been Julian's idea.

He might have crapped out on his friends in the end, but he deserved a small piece of the very large pie. The bulk of the money he'd received, he'd used to pay off the debts accumulated during the years after Alyssa's car accident.

In reality, it had been his mother's car accident that caused his sister's traumatic brain injury. He rarely talked about it, but he owed Kendall answers for his past behavior, and ripping open this particular vein was the only way to provide them.

They walked into his apartment, and Steve greeted them from his crate, prancing in circles, whining at the sight of them.

"Hey, man!" Julian let him out and accepted the nudging on his legs and the jumping, which ended with the dog's front legs and paws stretched against him. "Need a walk?" he asked the dog.

"That's rhetorical," he said, glancing at Kendall. "Want to come with me?"

"Sure thing." She was used to putting the dog's needs first, before settling herself.

He hooked Steve up to his leash and took him for a walk, during which their conversation was light. He obviously was saving the heavy stuff, and Kendall respected that. They returned to the apartment after half an hour, and he let Steve roam free. The dog grabbed a toy bone and settled into a corner by the couch. She was happy to see he'd settled in so well.

Kendall chose the corner of the sofa, while Julian walked to the big floor-to-ceiling window overlooking the street, up high enough to be private and give him a spectacular view of the city. He leaned against the glass and stared out until his vision blurred.

She knew he'd talk when he was ready, and she sat in silence, waiting.

"My father walked out when I was nine. About a year after my sister was born," he said, starting at the beginning.

"Wow, there are so many years between you. Lexie and I are, like, minutes apart. Both aren't typical."

He laughed. "No, not typical at all. In my case, apparently that's what happens when your parents fight all the time and have to find a way to make up. Alyssa was an accident."

Something she'd been reminded of by his mother. Often.

He glanced at Kendall, who watched him, the understanding in her gaze giving him the strength to continue. "After Dad left, my mother turned to alcohol to numb the pain, but she was really good at hiding it, working and raising us through her addiction."

He didn't recall the small apartment he'd grown up in fondly. They were tight quarters, and Alyssa, a colicky, crying baby, stayed in his mother's room while Julian slept on a pullout sofa in the den. With his grandparents' help, they'd moved to a place where he had his own room, which he'd eventually given up for his sister, returning to the sofa. But he knew there were people worse off, and he'd worked his ass off to get a scholarship so he could go away to school.

"My mother wasn't neglectful. She kept a roof over our heads and food on the table. And her parents helped raise us, so I guess, all in all, things weren't awful."

"Really?" Kendall asked, sounding angry, he guessed on his behalf. "Because it doesn't sound wonderful to me. That's like me saying my childhood was just fine because my father made sure we had a home and food to eat, regardless of the fact that my mother spent her entire life in a dark bedroom suffering from depression."

"I didn't realize that," he said, turning to face her. She was stronger than he'd ever been. "I'm sorry."

Her eyes softened. "Thank you, and we'll talk about it one day, but let's stay on you."

He smiled wryly. "Not letting me off the hook, are you?"

She shook her head. "Nope. You're giving me the facts but not the feelings behind them. And if we're going to get anywhere, I need both."

He blew out a deep breath, allowing the feelings he used to numb with drugs to come back. "It sucked, okay? I always smelled the alcohol on her breath. She had a hard time getting out of bed in the morning. I would catch her pouring vodka into her coffee for a jump start. So I got used to looking out for my sister, first when she was a baby and then as she got older. I felt responsible for her. She was such a tiny thing." He smiled at the memory. "And despite the age difference, we were close."

He leaned an arm against the window, glancing down at the lights and moving cars below. "I went to college when she was ten, and it was the hardest thing I've ever done, leaving her with my mother." He'd felt so damned guilty, as if him being there could have prevented what happened.

"Kids grow up, right? I'm sure your mom wanted you to go to school, get your degree?" Kendall asked.

He shook his head. "She didn't give a shit. But my grandparents did. They encouraged me, promised they'd be there for Alyssa. So I went."

"And you met Kade, Lucas, and Derek?"

He couldn't help but grin at the recollection. "We came up with this idea for a social media app while we were drunk one night and started to hash it out for real the next day, and the day after... and the day after. We knew we had something real."

He still remembered the high of those days, the comradery with the guys. How awesome he'd felt, how much he'd looked forward to the future.

"What happened?" Kendall asked.

He didn't meet her gaze. He knew he had to just keep talking and get it all out. "One night I got a call. It was my junior year, right before Christmas. We were due to go home for break soon. My mother was driving drunk and she had an accident. She hit a tree head on. She was killed instantly."

"Oh, Julian." Kendall came up behind him and wrapped her arms around him tight.

He didn't realize how much he needed her close—the warm, fragrant scent he associated with her and the strength she gave him now. "Alyssa was in the car. She wasn't wearing a seat belt. She was thrown from the seat, in a coma for a month, and suffered from a traumatic brain injury."

Kendall sucked in a startled breath. "I had no idea."

He swallowed hard. "No one did. I didn't tell anyone."

"Not Kade or any of the guys?"

"Nope. I was too mortified by what my mother had done. Too worried to share. I went home for Christmas, and I didn't want to go back. My grandparents convinced me. They said I needed the college diploma to get a job, to support myself and my sister, and they were right."

He swallowed over the lump in his throat. "And they stepped up even more, took on Alyssa's care when I wasn't home, and drained their bank accounts because my mother, it turns out, had let her health insurance lapse. And the bills were enormous."

"Wow."

Kendall wrapped her arms tighter, and suddenly the past didn't seem so daunting to tell. "I went back to school, but I couldn't deal with the pain and the worry. About Alyssa, her recovery, what her future would hold."

"So you started partying. And doing drugs." Her hand slipped up his back and began circling in gentle, supportive strokes.

"Guess it's not such big a leap to make."

"No," she murmured, resting her head on his shoulder as she continued to comfort him. "Tell me the rest of it."

He sighed, tipping his head against the cool window. "Isn't it obvious? I got hooked and told myself I wasn't. It numbed the pain. And what did it get me?" he asked bitterly, angry at himself.

"I pushed away the best friends I ever had, lost out on working on a revolutionary application, not to mention a billion-dollar IPO. Eventually I pulled my head out of my ass and got clean." The why of that was another ugly story for another day, Julian thought.

"But did being sober make me a good human being? No. I still went after Kade and Blink, used *you*, because all I could think about was saving my family from debt and destruction. Because I felt so guilty that I stupidly gave up that opportunity for addiction, I did things I still can't comprehend."

"Hey." She turned him toward her, and in her eyes, he didn't see disgust or condemnation.

He got a solid glimpse of understanding he still wasn't sure he deserved, but knew he desperately wanted and needed.

"We all make mistakes," she insisted, her pretty blue eyes begging him to believe.

"We all make *choices*," he immediately corrected her.

She inclined her head. "Whatever you want to call them, we're still entitled to forgiveness."

"Even me?"

She cupped his face between her soft palms, her gaze steady on his. "Especially you," she murmured, leaning in close until her lips brushed over his.

Chapter Six

KENDALL HADN'T PLANNED the kiss. She merely wanted Julian to know he was forgiven, that he deserved to put the past behind him just like she had. But she also needed to be close to him. And so she acted on impulse, but not the dangerous kind that led her into trouble, the kind that was born of deep need. If temptation did cause her trouble, only time would tell.

She'd meant to comfort, but the fire between them was still there, burning strong. Their mouths fused and desire burst free. Their sexual relationship had been hot, and clearly that hadn't changed.

He grasped her hair, winding his hand through the long strands, and tilted her head to one side. Her mouth opened, and his tongue slid inside, tangling with his, her entire body softening. Her breasts, full and heavy, pressed against his hard chest, but he was focused on her mouth.

He held her head in place and kissed her, over and over, lips gliding over hers, his thumb caressing her cheek. She moaned, and he broke the kiss, sliding his finger across her damp bottom lip.

Feeling naughty, she slicked her tongue out and licked his thumb.

"That's my kitten."

A full-body shiver took hold at the endearment, her nipples puckering into hardened peaks. The old Kendall, the brazen, brave, un-medicated Kendall, would have had her shirt off in an instant, her own hands cupping her breasts, offering herself to him. But now she was more sober and, it seemed, more thoughtful. The notion of playing that way embarrassed her more than anything. Sex didn't feel as wild and free.

"Hey. Where did you go?" He trailed his wet finger down her cheek, over her jaw, nudging her head up to look at him.

"I was thinking about us. Before. I'm not the same person. I don't feel the same. I don't act the same. It's the meds," she felt compelled to explain.

Maybe he wouldn't want her this way.

Maybe he expected the wild, uninhibited version of Kendall Parker. She ducked her head, not wanting to see the disappointment in his face.

"One question," he said, nudging her chin up so she had to meet his gaze.

She blinked up at him, waiting.

"Do you feel? When I kiss you?" He brushed his

lips over hers, nipping at her bottom lip.

Sensation shot from the sting of his bite to her swollen sex. "Yes," she murmured.

A satisfied smile lifted his lips into a seductive grin. "How about this?" He reached out and tweaked her nipple through her shirt.

Once again, sweet pain reverberated to her clit, and she answered with a soft groan.

"You do feel. You want me. That's what matters. Not the past. We're getting to know each other again and everything is new."

"You aren't... disappointed that I'm not jumping you where we stand?" she asked.

He cupped her face in his hand. "We're both different people, baby."

"Not kitten?" She didn't know whether to be sad or not that he'd let the nickname go.

"Starting fresh, remember?"

It was her turn to smile. "I do."

He swept her hair off one shoulder, bent down and kissed her jaw, licked his way upward, until he nibbled her ear, causing ripples of awareness to shoot through her veins. He worked his way back toward her mouth with soft, gentle kisses that felt like butterflies' wings against her skin. Arousal hummed low in her belly, and every whisper of his mouth, each lick of his tongue helped her insecurities and worry to flee under his attentiveness.

She pulled his shirt out from the waistband of his pants and slid her hands onto his bare skin, reveling in the feel of his warm flesh against hers. He shivered beneath her touch, building her courage along with her desire.

And when he lifted the hem of her dress, skimming his roughened palms over her thighs, she was ready for that step. He raised her dress and pulled it up and over her head, leaving her clad in a light blue lace bra and matching panties.

He let out a low whistle. "You take my breath away."

She felt his lust and approval everywhere and reached for his shirt, removing it and baring his muscular chest. She leaned forward and brushed her lips over his hair-roughened skin, inhaling his masculine scent, letting it settle inside her and wrap her in desire.

He sucked in a shallow breath and tugged her panties down her legs. She kicked them off and her bra came next. A flick of his wrist and she was removing the garment and adding it to the pile on the floor.

He turned her so her back was against the floor-to-ceiling window, easing her against the cool glass. The rush of cold against her skin was in stark contrast to the heat of desire flushing her from the inside out.

"Don't move."

She eagerly waited while he stripped off what remained of his clothing, his dark jeans and boxer briefs ending up on the floor. She took in his lean, muscular body, her gaze traveling from the chest she'd kissed down to the thick, solid erection.

He grasped her arms and placed them above her head, holding both in one strong hand. Her heart pounded hard in her chest, anticipation welling as she realized he wouldn't be taking her to the bed but *taking her* right here.

She drew her tongue over her lips. "I like your version of starting fresh." Her breasts ached, and her sex felt both full and empty at the same time, but her need wasn't just for physical fulfillment. She needed *him*.

"I missed you." He cupped a hand against her hip, then ran his palm up her side, following her curves, ending at the slope of her breast, his thumb stroking the full flesh of one globe, inching closer to her nipple.

She trembled with desire. Instinct had her reaching for him, her fingers itching to curl in his hair, but he held on tight to her wrists, keeping her in place.

"This is about you. Your pleasure. Your desire." He rubbed his finger back and forth across one nipple.

Shockwaves of need darted between her thighs. Dampness moistened her sex, and she arched her hips forward, a shameless plea for more. For his touch, his fingers, his cock… she'd take them all.

Dipping his head, he remained focused on her breasts. He released her arms and pushed them together, suckling on her nipples, first one, then the other, then back again. Alternating between light nips of his teeth and soothing strokes of his tongue. Her hips began to gyrate, to move in circles, desperate for the hard pressure of his cock against her sex, anything to relieve the ache he created.

He knew. He reacted, sliding his hand over her stomach, his fingers smoothly moving down her sex, to her slick lips, but he avoided her clit, the place where she needed his touch the most.

"You're teasing me," she said, frustrated.

"No, I'm pleasuring you." He swiped his tongue over her nipple once more, at the same time sliding a finger deep inside her. Her core contracted around him, and he added one more.

A small whimper released from the back of her throat. As he pumped his fingers in and out, sensual waves of desire built higher, and when he pressed hard on her clit, she shattered, coming apart in his talented hands. She was shocked at how quickly she'd reacted, how long the orgasm went on, and he maintained contact with her throughout, drawing out the sensual pleasure he gave.

As she came back to herself, he held her upright,

nuzzling her neck, patiently caring for her until she was on solid ground.

"Condom," he said, taking a step back and disappearing into the other room before returning quickly, packet in hand.

She was still catching her breath from her first orgasm when he returned and rolled the condom onto his thick shaft. He braced her face between his hands and kissed her hard, letting her know without a doubt how much he wanted her. Her body responded, desire beginning another slow, simmering build inside her.

He broke the kiss and her lips felt used and swollen.

"I didn't think we'd be back together like this," he said in a gruff voice. One that held a hint of gratitude, too.

"Me, either." She sunk her hands into his hair at last.

"I won't take it for granted."

She felt his words for the promise they were. And then she felt him, the head of his cock slipping between her thighs.

He lifted her easily, and she wrapped her legs around his waist as he pulled her down on his waiting shaft. As he slid inside her, her inner walls clamped tight around him. He was thick and full inside her, providing a respite from the ache he caused, but not complete relief.

"Move," she whispered, kissing from his jaw to his mouth, razor stubble abrading her lips as she glided across his skin.

"Whatever you want, baby." He braced her against the window and began to thrust.

She gasped and placed her hands on his shoulders, absorbing the impact with every muscle, every fiber of her being wrapped up in the sensual onslaught taking over her body. He picked up a rhythm she quickly became attuned to, hitting all the right spots, causing her desire and need to spike higher.

"Julian." She said his name on a moan, her body trembling, on the edge of release.

Without warning, he shifted position, lifting her leg higher, and his cock hit deeper inside her.

"God, Julian!" She cried out his name once more, lost to sensation.

He continued to thrust into her until white dots of light sparkled behind her eyes and her entire being was consumed by an explosive orgasm that shook her to the depths of her soul. "Oh, oh, oh!"

"That's it, baby, come hard for me."

She dug her nails into his back, holding on as she came, the shuddering waves seeming to go on forever. Just as the contractions racking her body began to subside, Julian thrust one last time and came with a groan.

"Kendall, baby. Fuck." He pounded inside her once, then twice more before stilling, his big body shaking against hers.

Dampness slickened his skin, and hers, as he finally separated them. She felt the loss of his body heat and thickness inside her.

"Come on." He bent and swept her into his arms, carrying her from the living room through the apartment and into his bedroom, depositing her onto his bed.

He walked to the bathroom, returning a few minutes later, and grabbed her naked body, pulling her into his arms. Without warning, the bed dipped, and she realized Steve had settled on the corner of the mattress along with them.

She grinned and snuggled against Julian, realizing he had never been a cuddler. Not before. But this was now, and they were starting fresh. And with that reality, her mind began to work again, and her thoughts came too fast and furiously for her liking.

Kendall had had a lot of sex in her past, more than she liked to think about, even if she now understood why she'd sought out that particular high. And this was the first time in her life she felt deeper emotions to go along with the physical act.

Even when she'd been with Julian before, it'd been

quick and fun, and any feelings she'd begun to develop for him had been separate from sex. Sex and sentiment were new to her, and she acknowledged the lump in her throat now as something serious. She'd recognized it during sex with Julian a little while ago. Even as her body had taken over and passion had overcome thought, she'd been aware that her emotions were engaged on a whole different level.

It hadn't taken long for him to work his way back into her heart in some way. And knowing the complications that came with any kind of relationship with this man, fear nearly paralyzed her. Instead she pushed herself away from him, nearly jumping off the bed in an attempt to escape.

★ ★ ★

ONE MINUTE JULIAN had Kendall in his arms, feeling satisfied and on the verge of dozing off. For a few blissful minutes, all had been right in his world. Then she'd stiffened, and he assumed her brain function had returned and panic had set in. He'd been prepared when she'd bolted from bed. Ready to grab her around the waist and pull her back down to the mattress.

He braced himself over her, his arms on either side of her shoulders.

Her eyes were wide, her breathing shallow.

"Kendall, look at me."

Big blue eyes settled on his face. "I can't do this. Don't you understand? Everything I've built, everything I need for stability could come crashing down around me."

Her words stabbed at his heart, but he understood where the fear was coming from. He'd always known if he ever wanted back into her life, he'd have some big dragons to slay in the form of his ex-best friend and Kendall's twin sister.

"I can't…"

He silenced her frantic panic with a soft, slow kiss, giving her something else to focus on. And for a few precious seconds, he could pretend they were two people with no ugly past.

He broke this kiss and touched his nose to hers. "Hear me out, okay?"

She nodded. "Okay. I'm sorry. I just freaked out."

"I get it. But let's make some decisions right here, right now."

She nodded. He rolled to the side, and she sat up beside him. They paused to pull down the comforter and climb under. Which meant she wasn't running.

"I take it you want to be here. You just are worried about the complications I bring to your life."

She bit down on her lush bottom lip. "Here's the thing. You might not realize this, but I don't have a lot of friends. What I have is my sister, who gave up most of her life to fix my messes. And that means I also have Kade and, by extension, the guys at Blink and their wives."

She drew a deep breath before continuing. "Now I'm not saying I don't want or intend to carve out my own place in life, but it would kill me to hurt the people who stood by me."

He couldn't argue with that. But he was just selfish enough to not want to let her go without seeing what could develop between them. He had a hunch she wanted the same thing or he wouldn't be so insistent now.

"Don't they want you to be happy?"

"Of course they do. They just won't think you're the one to make me that way. And up until a few days ago, neither did I."

He took that, accepted it, because he'd earned those feelings. "How about this. You give us time to explore what this"—he gestured between them—"is. For all we know, it'll fizzle out."

He doubted it.

But he went with it anyway. Anything to keep her calm. "Maybe you won't like my bad habits." Not that he intended to have any while he was convincing her they belonged together.

To his relief, her breathing had evened out. She was calmer.

"So what do you say?" His goal was to bind them close, so they could face her sister and his one-time friend together.

"I can do that," she murmured.

He let out a long breath, relieved he didn't have to fight her, too.

★　★　★

KENDALL ARRIVED AT work Monday morning to find daisies in a vase on her desk. She looked around for Josie, but she was obviously in the back with the dogs, so Kendall put her bag on the desk and searched for a card on the flowers. She found a small envelope taped to the back of the glass container.

She pulled out the paper and read the note. "Pretty flowers for my pretty girl. Julian." A warm fluttering took up residence in her stomach. This wasn't the same man she'd known. At least, she didn't think so.

He was attentive in a way he hadn't been before, and so much more caring. She felt awful for freaking out on him after the first time they'd had sex and, worse, for admitting she was afraid of the family conflict that would ensue if Kade and Lexie found out she was seeing him.

But it was her life, and she had to make her own choices and figure things out on her own. And she wanted to see where things with Julian could go.

She grabbed her phone and texted Julian. *Thank you for the flowers. XO* She bit the inside of her cheek and backspaced over the *XO*. Not yet.

Two seconds later, his answer came. *My pleasure. Thinking of you while busy in boring conference calls.*

She smiled and put the phone aside. She tucked the card into her handbag and settled in at her desk, getting lost in paperwork for a while before Josie came back.

They talked for a bit, then Josie made phone calls and Kendall returned to the never-ending forms and filing the job entailed.

Her iPhone rang, and she glanced down to see Lexie's name on the screen. She picked it up on the first ring. "Hi," she said to her twin.

"Hi yourself. How are you?"

"I'm good. Just working. You?"

"The same. I didn't speak to you this weekend. Is everything all right?" her sister asked.

Guilt rose up in her throat. "Yes. I was just busy. I had some clients who were away, and I walked a few more dogs than usual. I was tired so I fell asleep early. Nothing major," she said, glancing at the flowers from Julian and hating the benign lies.

Lexie was obviously calling to check up on her, and while Kendall understood it, she really wanted to have just one conversation where *how are you* wasn't code for *are you taking your meds and feeling okay?*

A part of her knew maybe she hadn't earned that yet, but another part of her felt that she had—and deserved that right more and more with every day that passed.

"Kendall? Are you there? I asked if you wanted to have lunch today," her twin said.

"Yes, that sounds good."

"I could come by the shelter. You know I love to see the dogs."

Kendall glanced at the flowers again and cringed. "Umm, okay," she said, not wanting to change their routine because her sister might wonder what Kendall was hiding.

Lexie did love to come by and see the dogs before their weekly lunches. "See you at twelve?" she asked.

"Sounds great!" Lexie disconnected the call.

And Kendall pressed her iPhone against her forehead.

"Problems?" Josie asked.

Kendall drew a deep breath. "Can I ask a favor?"

"Of course!" her boss said. She studied her, concerned. "What is it?"

"Can we put the flowers on your desk and, if my sister comments, just make like they're yours? I'm really sorry but… Oh God. It's a long story, but she wouldn't approve of Julian, and I'm trying to see if he's changed, and we need time before Lexie finds out about him being back in my life."

Josie nodded in understanding. "Of course I'll do it. It's not like you're asking me to commit murder or something." She smiled, rose, and picked up the vase, placing it on her desk. "They're so pretty. Not your usual flower. Just a sweet gesture," she said.

"I know." When Kendall pushed aside the concerns and let herself just be, she really enjoyed and appreciated the sentiment.

She felt a silly grin lift her mouth.

"Someone has it bad."

She blushed and shook her head. "I need to get back to work."

Josie laughed. And they dug into another hour's worth of phone calls and forms before the front door opened and Lexie walked in.

"Kendall!" Her twin walked straight to her and pulled her into a hug.

"Hi, Lex." She embraced her back.

"You two really are identical," Josie murmured. "Every time I see you, I can't get over it."

They laughed, used to people's reactions since they were little girls.

"Can I see the puppies?" Lexie asked.

Kendall gestured to the back door. "Of course."

Together they headed to the pens, pausing by each

so Lexie could bend down and talk to the dogs.

They reached the third pen from the end, and Lexie paused. "Where's Steve?"

She hesitated, then said, "He finally got a new owner. One I know will take good care of him." And no need to elaborate on who that owner just happened to be.

"I'm glad. I'll miss seeing him, but he's so much better off. I just wish I could have taken him," Lexie said, sounding sad. She'd always, like Kendall, had a soft spot for the gray pooch.

"Eventually Kade will give in," Kendall said of her brother-in-law's insistence that they couldn't have a dog because of the pet hair. Kade was a touch OCD. "You can get a mix that has poodle in it. Or go to a breeder if you must, and get a non-shedding breed."

Despite them being alone, Lexie leaned in close and whispered in Kendall's ear. "I think he's going to have to get used to a baby, first."

"What? You're kidding! Oh my God!" Kendall threw her arms around her sister, genuinely thrilled. "You're going to be a mom and I'm going to be an aunt!"

Her sister hugged her back. "You're going to be an awesome aunt. Now how about we feed me? I'm starving and I'm eating for two."

Kendall paused, taking a long look at her sister's so

similar features. "I love you, Lex." She knew part of her sentimentality came from the guilt of keeping secrets from the one person she'd always told the truth.

Still, the warmth and high from her time with Julian remained, and she couldn't deny how badly she wanted things between them to be real this time. And if it meant keeping the truth from her sister for a little while, she'd just have to live with the deception.

Chapter Seven

JULIAN PULLED UP at the floral shop where his sister worked, not far from where he used to live. Thanks to the Blink settlement, Alyssa lived in an apartment a few blocks over, in a nice neighborhood he felt comfortable with her walking to and from, day or night. She lived alone, and he'd learned to be fine with that. He still worried about her much more than he needed to.

He was looking forward to taking her to lunch and catching up. Despite the age difference, he'd always felt close to her. Maybe it was the circumstances in which they'd grown up, maybe it was his protective nature, or maybe it was biology. She was his baby sister and always would be.

He walked in to find her wearing a dark-colored apron, scissors in one hand, flowers in another, humming while she worked. The sight of her doing everyday things never failed to warm his heart, bringing him back to a time he wasn't sure she'd have a normal life.

"Julian!" Her face lit up as she caught sight of him.

"Just let me finish up and I'll be ready to go." She snipped another stem on the flowers and set them into a vase before removing her apron and washing her hands in a back sink. "Kate," she called out to her boss.

The unique woman with pink stripes in her hair stepped out from the back of the shop. "Oh, your handsome brother is here!"

They'd met before, and her boss was harmless, just flirty. She was eccentric, and her work ethic did well with Alyssa's needs. She let her set a schedule she could handle, didn't throw surprise requests her way, and accepted the occasional slow speech when she couldn't access a word she ought to know.

"How are you?" Kate asked.

"I'm fine. And you?"

She smiled. "All's well here, thanks to my star employee. Your sister has a talent for arrangements." She glanced at Alyssa and waved a hand. "Go. Take your lunch. I'll see you later."

Julian waited for Alyssa to join him up front. "How are you, squirt?" he asked, always using her childhood nickname.

She rolled her eyes. "When are you going to remember I'm an ad... ad... adult?" she said, adjusting the end of the sentence to the slow, measured speech she'd adopted after the accident and learned at therapy. Sometimes normal words came hard for her, either to say or remember.

"You're always going to be my baby sister."

"Well, your baby sister wants sushi for lunch."

"Whatever you want." His hand twitched to ruffle her hair, but he refrained. No twenty-one-year-old wanted her older brother to treat her like a kid.

Over lunch, they shared a variety of rolls and normal talk. "I love this job. It's so much better than the last shop I worked in. Kate is so amaz... amazing to work with." She tucked her dark brown hair behind one ear.

Alyssa hadn't gone to college. She'd nixed the offer when Julian made it, even if they'd had to take out loans for her to go. But she said it was too hard, her brain no longer worked that way, and she was okay with that. More than he was, since it had always been in her grand plan before the accident. Instead she wanted to focus on creative things that fed her soul and made her happy. Julian was completely on board, and now he had the means to help support her when needed.

"I'm glad."

"So what's new with you?" Alyssa asked before popping a spicy tuna roll into her mouth.

"Well, I have news. I'm seeing someone." He hadn't told Alyssa the last time he'd been with Kendall, but everything this time was more serious.

"Julian, you have a girlfriend?" His sister's green eyes, similar to his own, sparkled back at him.

"I do." Although it felt weird to call Kendall that because all his prior women had been hookups, that's what she was.

"Will I get to meet her?"

"Do you want to?"

She straightened her shoulders. "I want to give my stamp of approval."

Julian shook his head and laughed. "You'll approve. I have no doubt." He grinned and felt the heat rush to his cheeks as he thought of Kendall.

A few minutes into his sushi, his iPhone buzzed, showing an incoming text from Kendall. "Dinner… and me. Any way you want. My place. Eight p.m."

His dick liked that suggestion if the hardening in his pants was anything to judge by. He immediately texted back. "With an offer like that, let's do you first and dinner after." He grinned and placed his phone on the table.

"Is that her?" Alyssa asked.

He nodded. Why deny it?

"You have it bad," his sister said, laughing. "And I like it. I want to come hang out with Steve, so I can meet her then."

"We'll set something up." He turned his attention

to his food, pleased his two best girls would finally meet.

A little while later, he paid the check and they left the restaurant. He'd walk her back to the flower shop before heading home for an afternoon's worth of computer and security work.

He left his sister securely inside her place of work and walked out the door, heading for his car. From the corner of his eye, he saw a flash of a woman's face and long light brown hair duck into the nearest alley.

He narrowed his gaze, feeling like he'd seen the girl before. He strode to the entry to the alley and glanced around, but no one was there.

He shrugged and headed home, finally feeling like he had something important to head home *to*.

★　★　★

AFTER THE NIGHT Kendall spent with Julian, and in the time she'd taken afterwards to come to terms with her new reality and how much she wanted things to work with him, she'd reached inside herself. And decided she wanted to resurrect parts of the Kendall she'd suppressed when she'd gone on medication and decided to be the perfect patient.

She took her time getting ready for Julian to arrive. First, a long, hot shower, where she luxuriated in her favorite crème-brulée-scented shower gel and followed up with matching/complementary moisturizer. She made certain to rub her hands up her freshly shaven legs, knees, and thighs, then follow up her arms, chest, and stomach. She wanted to smell good enough to eat so he'd act on the impulse.

She chose a simple short dress that was as easy to take off as it was to put on and left her feet bare.

As for dinner, she wasn't a good cook. She'd never slowed down enough to learn, so she ordered in food from a gourmet shop down the street. Her kitchen was small, but she set the table and added candles, an intimate touch she'd never tried before.

"Ready for company?" she asked Waffles. "I have a surprise for you." Julian had texted and asked if he could bring Steve. Apparently the dog had grown attached to him since he worked from home.

Just as she put dinner in the oven to heat, the doorbell rang, and she rushed over to answer, Waffles by her side, dancing and barking. "Shh."

A glance through the peephole showed her guests had arrived. She held on to Waffle's collar as she opened the door and didn't let go until they stepped inside.

"Hey, baby." Julian grabbed her around the waist, pulling her close. His hard body aligned with hers, the thick outline of his cock pressing against her belly as he placed a long kiss on her lips. Her stomach fluttered with immediate wanting, desire rolling through her body. "I missed you," he said, breaking the kiss.

"I missed you, too."

He bent down, giving her an unobstructed view of his tight ass in faded jeans, and unhooked Steve's leash because the dog was pulling so he could wrestle with Waffles. He rose back to standing. "Go. Play."

"Welcome," she said, waving them into her apartment. "I'm sure the two dogs will settle down in a little while," she said of the animals playing, running from the entry to the family room and back again.

Julian grinned. "I like to see him playful and happy. I especially think he's got good taste, picking a female in the Parker family as his new girl."

She touched his cheek, then spun away. "Come. I have dinner for us." She led him into the kitchen, where she had chicken Marsala and sautéed broccoli ready for them.

"Did you cook this?"

"Nope. Don't get your hopes up that you're involved with a chef or anything. Lots of takeout and basic eating here. How about you?"

He shrugged. "I can do a little more than the basics. I used to cook for Alyssa when my mother wasn't up to it."

She met his gaze. "My sister and I used to make spaghetti when our mom was too depressed to leave her room." She caught herself, having already decided she wanted tonight to be light and fun, not serious and intense, and changed the subject. "So if you want pasta, I can boil water. But I figured it wasn't good date night food."

"Oh, I don't know. Lady and the Tramp made it work."

She laughed. "Comparing us to the dogs, now?"

He chuckled but had no good comeback.

She plated the food while he watched, then he placed the dishes on the table.

The dogs had settled in beside each other in the family room, playing nicely with toys. She and Julian began to eat, talking about everyday things, television shows, movies, and things they discovered they had in common.

Soon she finished the delicious chicken, and he did the same, sliding the plate away from him.

"I'm full and that was excellent," he murmured.

She nodded in agreement. "How's work?" she asked.

"Busy. New clients are lining up. With hacking becoming so prevalent, my business is doing well, for which I'm grateful."

"That's great."

He nodded. "I've hired outside consultants and people who work directly for me. I'm growing. What about you? How's the job going?"

She blew out a slow breath. "I love working with dogs. I get so much satisfaction placing homeless dogs with their perfect people." Her tone dropped a bit.

"But? I can hear it in your voice."

"It's not a job that gives me enough of an income to fully support myself. And the longer I'm out of the hospital and on my own, the more I know it's time to find something more permanent."

"Do you have any ideas?" he asked.

She hesitated for a good long while, and he gave her the space she needed to work up the courage to admit her goals.

Finally, she spoke. "I really want to be a vet tech. I'd need two years at a veterinary technology School accredited by New York State. There are a few local schools that would work and some that are in the suburbs. I could take the train... or rent an apartment there."

"You've thought this through." His eyes gleamed with approval.

"I've already met with an admissions counselor at one of them. I can go part time and not have to quit my job." And the thought of having her own steady income, a goal she could work toward, gave her a feeling of pride.

"Then do it. I know you can make it happen."

"Really? You believe in me?"

He grasped her face in his hands. "I definitely believe in you."

She couldn't help the smile that took hold. "You're the only one I've told. I haven't even let Lexie know. Or my father."

And she'd have to ask him for a loan. Or, he'd insist on paying. Her father was an investment banker who could more than afford to cover the cost of school. But he'd done so much for her over the years, and even if he'd put the brunt of her care on her twin, financially he'd always been there.

"I'm glad you trusted me with your hopes and dreams," Julian said.

She smiled. "Me, too." She glanced at their empty plates. "Can I get you anything else?" she asked.

His eyes darkened, and she recognized the desire that filled them. "Just you."

★ ★ ★

As JULIAN LISTENED to Kendall talk about her future, a mixture of admiration and longing rushed through him—a desire that surpassed the physical for a woman he was coming to want more with each passing day.

He held out his hand, and she grasped it, curling her fingers around his. He pulled her toward him, and she came willingly, ending up in his lap, her legs straddling his on the chair. Her dress hiked up her thighs, exposing her delicate panties, and the warm heat of her sex settled against his hard cock. Ripples of awareness trickled through his veins.

She slid her arms around his neck and sighed. "How did we get here?" she asked.

"I got fucking lucky," he muttered before sealing his lips over hers.

He slipped his tongue inside her mouth and lost himself in her taste, her sweetness, everything that was Kendall. And she met him halfway, moaning when he swept inside, tongues tangling in an effort to bring them as close as possible.

Her body rocked against his thick erection, and he lifted her dress, slipping a hand up her back, guiding her back and forth as her hips moved enticingly against him. Her soft sighs breathed into his mouth, the noises growing louder as her hips gyrated faster over his denim-covered dick.

He broke the kiss, stroking the soft skin on her back, urging her on.

"Mmm," she murmured, kissing him again while clearly working up to an orgasm.

"That's it, baby. Take what you need." His cock was hard, his balls tight, but his focus was on her pleasure.

And just when he thought he couldn't stand to not

be inside her warm, wet body, she stiffened against him, then trembled in his arms as she came apart, her orgasm going on and on. He fought against coming himself, waiting until she'd ridden out her enjoyment before standing with her in his arms.

She wrapped her legs around his waist, and he strode out of the kitchen and into the family room. The dogs had crashed, sleeping curled into each other on Waffles bed on the floor.

Julian shook his head and passed by them, heading straight for her bedroom. He lay her on the bed and stepped back to undress. While he stripped bare, she pulled her dress over her head, revealing a skimpy matching set of bra and panties, which he paused to admire for half a second before she tossed them onto the floor.

She turned, crawling up to the head of the bed, giving him a perfect view of her delectable ass. Acting on impulse, he placed a well-timed slap on her rear before she could turn back around.

"Hey!" she squealed, and he wasn't sure if she was reacting to the contact or the sound. She glanced over her shoulder, her eyes darkening.

In their earlier relationship, they'd experimented a little. He'd tied her arms and legs during sex, and she'd loved it. He'd lightly slapped her ass, and she'd come quickly right after. Not to mention what it'd done to him, amping up his desire, just as he felt now.

He rubbed the red, heated mark he'd left behind on her ass, and she moaned at his touch. Although some things had changed, and she was mellower, other things hadn't—their physical and emotional connection and their enjoyment of fun sex.

He slapped her other cheek. She arched her back, lifting her ass toward his palm, not away from it. His own body was throbbing with a need that increased every time she responded to his actions. He rubbed the newly reddened area, and she glanced at him, over her shoulder, her lashes fluttering, her eyelids heavy with desire.

"Don't move." He reached for his pants on the floor and pulled out a condom, unwrapping it and drawing it onto his aching shaft.

She wiggled her ass in reply, earning her another light slap. Her answering sensual moan went straight to his dick. He needed to be inside her. Yesterday.

Bracing a hand on her sleek lower back, he guided his cock into her sex, sliding his shaft along her wet pussy before he notched the head inside her.

"Ooh," she moaned, a sound he felt everywhere.

Inch by gratifying inch, he glided into her wet heat until he was balls deep. So fucking *deep*.

"Oh, Julian."

"Right here, baby." His name on her lips caused

his desire to kick up a notch higher, and he hadn't thought that was possible. Not when his body was wired and already slick with desire and sweat. The only thing keeping him from coming was the urge to make sure she climaxed first.

He wrapped his hand around her hair and tugged, eliciting a shuddering moan. He slid his cock out and thrust back in, finding his own rhythm, one she matched, grinding back against him with each successive thrust inside her.

She shook and trembled, searching for the ultimate fulfillment. He slid one arm around her waist and pressed a finger on her clit, moving it in a circular motion, his fingertip wet with her desire. A few more strokes and she came around him, moaning incoherent words in between sobbing out his name.

Only then did he let go, allowing her climax to trigger his own. He began to pump into her, grasping her hips and plunging deep, over and over again. The aftermath of her orgasm caused her inner walls to clasp his dick in a moist, tight tunnel. He'd never felt anything so hot, so right.

"Oh, fuck, Kendall." He came on a shout, lost to the hot spurts leaving his cock and the waves of pleasure tackling his body.

A little while later, they were cuddled beneath the covers, something he couldn't remember doing with her in the past. This need to stay close to any woman, and to her in particular, was new to him.

He held her close, inhaling her warm, fragrant scent that was delicious. He nuzzled his nose into her neck and shoulder, licking behind her ear, and she giggled.

"Silly."

"I'm just happy." And he was, which was a unique feeling for him.

"Why? What makes you happy right now?" she asked.

He drew a deep breath. "You. And the fact that you still trust me or you wouldn't let me spank you."

"We click sexually," she murmured. "But yes," she admitted. "I'm coming to trust you. Not again, because I just can't think about the past as something that was honest. Or real. But I'm coming to trust you now."

It was fucking amazing to hear those words from her beautiful lips. He didn't kid himself. They had a truckload of obstacles ahead of them in the form of her family. But for this moment in time, he had everything he wanted.

★   ★   ★

THE NEXT MORNING, Julian left Kendall's early because he had a conference call, but not before he'd claimed her once more. If he was in the room with her, he desired her. That wasn't new. What had changed was the realization that there was so much more between them than sex.

No, it hadn't been that long since she'd forgiven him, but in that short time, he'd opened himself up to her. Been honest about himself and his past, and he hadn't been disappointed. She'd accepted him, faults, flaws, and all. Leaving her this morning hadn't been easy, but it was necessary.

He walked out of her building with Steve on a leash. The dog hadn't left his new girlfriend without a fight. He'd cried as Julian put his leash on and dragged him away from Waffles.

He stopped at a corner café to grab a cup of coffee, and it took awhile before a taxi willing to pick up Julian and Steve stopped for them. The ride was short, the sun hot through the back window, as Steve pressed his nose against the glass during the trip.

Julian hadn't gotten much sleep last night, and that was okay with him. He had a damned good reason. The woman he'd left sleeping in her bed, hair tousled over her pillow and face, a soft smile on her lips when he'd kissed her good-bye.

"We're here," the driver said, pulling up to the curb by Julian's apartment.

He slid his credit card into the slot and handled the

payment and a nice tip for taking Steve, too, before climbing out of the cab. He was walking across the sidewalk into his building when he heard his name. It was a soft whisper, but it was enough for him to turn.

A young girl with long, dark curly hair met his gaze. Her hands were shoved into the pockets of a hooded, zippered sweatshirt that had seen better days, and her jeans were ripped and faded. But it was her eyes that triggered his instant recall.

"Alex?"

"You ... you remember me?"

She was older now, her hair longer, her expression sadder. But her vivid eyes were so light green they often appeared blue. Just like her brother's.

"Of course I do. Billy's sister," he said of his one-time friend, although drug buddy would be a better term.

During the time after college when Julian was high more often than not, he'd hung around with Billy and his group of friends. Julian was lazy and didn't do much beyond drugs and occasionally showing up for whatever menial labor job he could find, but Billy had been more hard-core.

He was currently doing time for possession and dealing, and his arrest had been the catalyst for Julian to clean up his act—because but for the grace of God, Julian could have been with him. And he couldn't have afforded to end up behind bars, abandoning his baby sister the way Billy had. Alex had been left with no one to fend for her, and she'd ended up in the foster care system.

He met her gaze. "How did you find me?"

She pulled her sweatshirt tighter around her, her hands never leaving her pockets. "I was wandering near where I used to live with Billy when I thought I saw you. You were busy with a woman and I didn't know if I should bother you."

"I knew someone was following me. Why didn't you say anything?"

"I had to work up the nerve," she mumbled. "Then I Googled your address on the computer at school."

She obviously had something she needed from him, and getting it out of her was going to be like pulling teeth. "Are you hungry? There's a place on the corner that makes killer pancakes."

Her eyes lit up. "I guess," she said, her casual words at odds with the longing in her expression. The kid was hungry.

He bit back a grin. "Let me take this guy upstairs and cancel my nine a.m. appointment and we'll go eat. And talk."

"Can I pet him?" she asked.

He nodded and while he pulled out his phone and

called a long-time client, Alex petted and talked to a very happy Steve. Luckily the client understood he had an emergency come up. They agreed to reschedule and touch base later. He ran upstairs and crated Steve, who was tired from his morning exertion. A cab ride was apparently a lot for the dog.

Julian returned to find Alex standing where he'd left her. "Ready?" He glanced at her, but she didn't rush to start walking. "What's wrong?" he asked.

"I don't have any money." Her cheeks burned with embarrassment.

"And I didn't ask you expecting you to pay. Now let's go eat. I want to know what's going on with you."

When she hesitated, he placed a hand on her back and nudged her forward until she was shuffling her way along with him.

A little while later, they were seated across from each other in a booth. Julian had handed her a plastic menu and told her to order whatever she wanted. If she hadn't ordered a large stack of pancakes, bacon, and orange juice, he'd have placed a similarly big order for her. His gut told him she was hungrier than she'd admit to being, which brought out the same protective instincts he'd have if his sister looked as lost and afraid.

"Why aren't you in school?" he asked, then realized, for all he knew, she'd graduated. "How old are you now, anyway?"

"Eighteen."

The waitress poured two cups of coffee, and he looked down, adding some cream to his.

"When do you graduate?" he asked her.

"Next year."

His gaze shot to hers. "Shouldn't you graduate this year?" he asked.

She swallowed hard, her eyes large and luminous in her face. "When Billy went… away, I got sent to foster care."

"I know." And if he'd been in any shape to help her, he would have.

At the time, he'd been addicted, and though he'd decided to kick the habit, it hadn't been an easy road. He'd holed up in a pay-by-the-day hotel, shivering and puking his way to sobriety. By the time he'd come out the other end, he'd been hanging on by a thread.

Determined to do right by his sister at last, he'd found an NA meeting. It hadn't been easy, admitting his addiction, fighting his demons, staying clean. And in the process, he'd all but forgotten about Billy's sister.

Guilt consumed him now, but he pushed it away, focusing on what he could fix. "What's going on?" he asked her.

She twirled a strand of hair around her finger…

around and around until she was pulling at the hair on her head. "In all the shuffling around with foster homes early on, I kind of lost a year. So I'm a junior."

He nodded. "And where are you staying now?" he asked. Because at eighteen, the system would be finished with her.

"I aged out, and my foster mother threw me out the door on my birthday a little over a month ago." She glanced down at the table, not meeting his gaze.

Fuck. He clenched his hands into a tight fist beneath the table, determined that she didn't see how upset her words made him. "Where have you been staying?"

"With a guy I know who aged out ahead of me. But his friends are druggie assholes."

Fuck and fuck.

Just then, the waitress came by with their meals. She placed the plates in front of them.

"Do you have a plan?" he asked when they were alone again.

Alex shook her head, tears in her eyes. "Last night they stole money I had saved from working after school. I won't go back there." She curled her hands into fists on the table. "I'll sleep in Central Park if I have to."

"So you came to me."

She shrugged. "You were always decent to me.

You didn't try and cop a feel like some of Billy's other friends. But if it's a hassle, I'll just go." She started to push herself out of her seat, her untouched meal in front of her.

"Wait."

His deep voice startled her and she bolted upright.

"Eat. Then you can stay with me until we figure something out."

Her shoulders slumped in sheer relief, and the tears hovering in her eyes fell onto her cheeks.

His stomach twisted in pain.

"You mean it?" she asked.

"I wouldn't offer if I didn't."

"Can I get you anything else?" the waitress asked.

He glanced at Alex's empty juice glass. "Some more OJ please."

The woman nodded and walked away.

"Why?" Alex asked.

"Why what?"

"Why are you helping me?"

He leaned closer, ignoring the delicious smell of his food and focusing on her instead. "Because I have a sister. And I'd like to think, if she needed help, someone would step up for her."

And because in some weird way, he felt like he owed her. For being selfish and not giving a thought to what would happen to her when her brother went to jail. Something else to add to his sins.

"But there's a catch," he said.

"Of course there is," she spat. "I'm leaving."

"No, you're listening. You'll finish school and graduate. And if you're working a part-time job, you'll keep it up." Which would keep her out of trouble.

She blew out a deep breath. "That's it?"

"Yeah. That's it."

Her shoulders slumped in relief, and he didn't want to ask what she'd *thought* his stipulation in exchange for giving her a place to stay would be.

He shook his head. He also knew he had to talk to Kendall and explain his new houseguest, but this was something he needed to do in person. And she was going to visit her parents today, something he knew was a stressful event for her.

With that discussion out of the way, Alex dug into her food. He noted she practically wolfed down her pancakes, which told him it'd been awhile since she'd had a decent meal.

"Any news from Billy?" he asked.

"He's getting out soon," she said before gulping down her drink.

Although this was good news for Billy, he didn't think the same held true for Alex. Or Julian, since she'd be staying at his place. He'd just have to take it one step at a time.

Chapter Eight

KENDALL SPENT HER day off from the shelter walking dogs and enjoying both the sunshine and the change in her life. Julian had risen early, kissing her into wakefulness, rolling her over and sliding inside her before she'd even processed his intent.

She'd gone from a lonely woman seeking friendship and fulfillment to the beginnings of finding those very things. She wasn't silly enough to think she had all the answers, but she'd made a start. A man who cared, who believed in her ability to start over with a new career. She could do these things if she put her mind to it. And she didn't have to do it alone.

Today she had the day off, so she planned on doing laundry and straightening up. Later that evening, Kendall, Lexie, and Kade descended on Kendall's parents' house to celebrate her father's birthday.

Kendall knew it was too much to hope that her mother, Addy, would come down to the kitchen for dinner and cake. And she arrived to find her mother was holed up upstairs. Basically she didn't leave the bedroom, and it was only in the last year that Kendall's

133

dad, Wade, had hired a live-in nurse to help him with his wife's situation. He didn't want to put her in a treatment facility or assisted living, and Kendall respected his decision. But nothing changed the fact that Kendall hadn't had a real mother for the better part of her life.

She'd already gone upstairs to say hello and kiss her mother's cheek, but she'd been in her rocking chair and hadn't responded. From past experience, Kendall knew it would take awhile for the pit that had lodged in her stomach to go away.

Her father always brought in dinner from a local restaurant, and tonight they'd eaten roast chicken, red potatoes, and green beans. Lexie had offered to pick up the cake, and Kendall had taken care of a joint gift, which was an Apple TV for him to stream new shows. He certainly had the time on his hands to watch.

They moved into the family room after cake and coffee, and Kade began the process of hooking up the Apple TV, leaving Lexie and Kendall talking with their father.

"Okay, enough about me. Tell me what's going on with each of you," Wade asked. "Kendall?"

She glanced at him. "Actually, I was thinking of going back to school." Thanks to Julian's positive reaction, she had the courage to share her news. "I want to be a vet tech."

"That's fabulous," Lexie said. "You'd be a perfect fit!"

"I agree," Kade said, approval and admiration in his gaze.

She was used to seeing compassion in Kade's expression, but his admiration filled her with pleasure and pride.

"I would love for you to go back to school!" her father said. "Can I help?"

Kendall smiled. "I'll let you know if and when I need anything, Dad. Thank you. For everything. All of you. I'm so grateful for your support. I can't tell you what it means to me to know I have you in my corner." She smiled, knowing how very fortunate she was.

"We love you, K."

"We do," her father added. "And now you, Lexie. What's going on? You seemed preoccupied at dinner."

"Well, now that you mention it... Kade and I have news," Lexie said.

Personally, Kendall didn't know how she'd held the exciting revelation in during dinner.

"What is it?" Wade asked.

"Lexie's having my baby," Kade said from behind the television set. He rose and strode out to where Wade was hugging Lexie.

"That's such wonderful news!" their father said, stepping back and studying his daughter with pride. "I can't wait to be a grandfather."

"It's awesome," Kendall agreed.

"I wish your mother… Never mind," her father said.

Lexie met his gaze. "I told her, Dad. When I went upstairs before dinner. No reaction," Lexie said, her voice cracking.

And that explained why Lexie had needed time to compose herself over dinner before telling their father the same news.

Kade pulled Lexie into his arms. "I'm over the moon." His voice was rough, and he couldn't take his gaze off his wife.

And not for the first time tonight, she was envious of her sister. Lexie had the ability to bring her husband around her friends and family without worrying about what anyone would say. Or think. Kendall longed for the same freedom. To go where she wanted, to bring Julian around her family. To just be who and what she was without judgment or condemnation.

As much as she understood why Lexie and Kade would lose their minds if they found out Kendall was seeing Julian, they didn't know him now. They didn't know what he'd been through in the past, how far he had come. How hard he was trying to be a better man. If she told them, would they care?

"So, Kendall…" Her father turned his attention to

her. "Any special man in your life?" he asked, as if on cue.

She swallowed hard. This was her chance. "No, no one in particular," she lied.

Not because she was a coward but because she didn't want to ruin Lexie's news with an argument, and because she wanted to talk to Julian before she took such a big step.

She'd have to keep her secret awhile longer and hope when her sister did discover the truth, she'd find it in her heart to understand and agree that people had the ability to change. And to want Kendall's happiness above anything else.

As for Kade, Kendall would have to rely on Lexie to persuade her husband to leave the past where it belonged and embrace the future.

★ ★ ★

AFTER LEAVING HER father's house, Kendall had planned to go straight home and spend the night alone. She had things to do at her apartment, like bookkeeping for her dog-walking business that she hadn't had time to finish this afternoon, and there was unfinished laundry to be folded. And as much as she loved being with Julian, she figured it was a smart idea to spend time alone, too.

Except after an evening with happily married, expecting-a-baby Kade and Lexie, Kendall had the urge to show up on Julian's doorstep and spend time with her own man. She also couldn't wait to share the positive response she'd gotten about her school plans from her family. It was a novel experience, to have someone other than Lexie to turn to when she had news.

Instead of heading home, she took a cab from Penn Station to Julian's apartment. She'd have to go home later because Waffles was alone, but she had time to stop for a visit.

She knocked on his apartment door, and he answered right away, wearing an old pair of sweats riding low on his hips and a gray tee shirt, his delectable forearms on display. Steve ran up by his side but waited politely behind the door. Julian had obviously been working on training, and she was impressed.

"Kendall!" he said, his shock evident in his voice and expression.

"Surprise!" She wrapped her arms around his neck and pulled him close, inhaling his seductive masculine scent.

After an evening of watching her sister and her husband be all cuddly and lovey-dovey celebrating her pregnancy, after not being able to share the real news she had of her own, that she and Julian had found... well, not love, not yet, but something real and with potential, she wanted to be as close to him as possible.

She braced her hands on his cheeks and pulled him in for a kiss, covering his mouth with hers and sliding her tongue between his parted lips. She was feeling particularly brazen and braver than she'd been in a while.

She broke the kiss, and he brushed her hair off her face. "Kendall, we need to talk."

"Later. I want you and I'm in no mood for conversation." She ran her hands over his shirt-covered chest, starting at his nipples, which puckered beneath her hands, then slid her palms to the waistband of his sweats.

His cock was thick, bulging behind the heavy cotton material, and her mouth watered at the thought of getting her mouth on him at last.

"Kendall—"

She pulled on the white tie holding up his sweats when he grasped her wrist.

"Are you playing hard to get?" she asked, leaning in to lick his bare chest.

"Is this your girlfriend?" a female voice asked.

"Who is that?" Kendall glanced behind Julian to see a young woman studying her with curiosity. "Is that your sister?" As Kendall asked, she started toward the girl.

"No, it's not. Look, like I said, we need to talk."

Kendall stiffened, suddenly unsure of herself and her place here. After all, she'd shown up unexpectedly, and she and Julian hadn't discussed exclusivity, but this girl was so *young*, and things between Kendall and Julian were so intense.

Trust.

Don't jump to conclusions, she warned herself, despite the fact that their rocky past was running through her mind and warning her to be careful.

"Okay... talk. Or introduce us." She gestured to the brunette watching them intently.

"Alex, can you give us some privacy?" he asked.

"Fine." She raised her hands in defeat and headed back toward... the bedrooms. Steve trotted after her.

"Where is she going? Better yet, what is she doing here? And who is she?" Kendall asked.

Julian placed his hand against the small of her back and led her toward the couch in the den. "Let's sit."

She stepped away and settled into the far corner of the sofa. Distance would enable her to hear what he had to say and process it without being distracted by his sexy nearness.

Julian sat down, twisting his hands. "Back in my drug days, I was friends with a guy named Billy Walker. Alex is his sister."

He looked to her for some reaction, but Kendall remained silent.

"Okay, well, as I was saying, I was friends with Billy. We used to… get high together… and he was my dealer. That was the extent of it for me but Billy was in deeper. Anything for a quick buck."

Kendall swallowed hard. "Go on."

"One afternoon, I met up with him to score. I had the shit in my pocket and all of a sudden, the cops came out of nowhere. I took off but the cops couldn't catch me. Billy got popped for dealing and possession. I skated and he went to jail." Julian shook his head.

Kendall blew out a sharp breath.

Julian went on. "Alex was left as a ward of the state. That was my wakeup call to get clean. Except… I was so wrapped up in withdrawal and my own problems I didn't give a thought to what happened to Alex."

Kendall tried to process his words and her feelings. Of course, she felt for the girl who'd lost her brother and ended up in foster care. "What's going on *now*?"

"She aged out of foster care and has nowhere to go. She was staying with some kids who got out before her, but it was a bad situation, a rough crowd. They stole the money she'd saved from working. And I don't think she's been eating much, either," he said, lowering his voice.

"She came here?"

He nodded. "I couldn't very well turn her out on

the street or send her back to where she came from, could I?"

"No," she breathed out, taking in the story and feeling sorry for the young girl.

She also saw yet another side to Julian. A caring, sensitive, selfless side. So opposite of the man who'd callously used her last year. More proof that he really had changed. Was different. More self-aware.

The man she used to know would never have taken in a young girl who had nothing to do with him today. He wouldn't feel guilty for leaving her behind to beat his addiction. This was the man she cared about.

"What are you thinking?" he asked.

"That I admire what you're doing for her." She felt the smile lift her lips. "That I admire you."

He blinked in surprise. "You're not upset that she's here?"

"What would it say about me if I was?" Kendall asked.

It was his turn to grin. "Thank you." He reached out and grabbed her hand, squeezing it tight.

"For what?" she asked.

"For believing in me." He met her gaze. "I'm not sure I remember the last time someone told me I did good."

She wrapped her arms around his neck, holding him close. Everyone should have someone who believed in them, she thought. Even at her worst, she'd had her twin. "You're doing the same for that girl. Let's call her back in so I can meet her."

Julian gazed at Kendall appreciatively, as if she'd hung the moon. "Alex!" he called. "There's someone I want you to meet."

An hour later, she'd spent time with the girl who, despite a crappy set of life circumstances, had managed to come out with a positive attitude and a good work ethic. She wanted to make something of herself, did well in school, and held down a part-time job in the afternoons. She'd kept her head down in foster care and lived with a decent enough family—at least until she no longer brought money in from the government.

And she definitely trusted Julian, while he clearly had a soft spot for her, too. He treated her like a little sister, which made Kendall even more eager to meet his real sibling and check out their dynamic for herself.

"I want to meet the dogs at your shelter," Alex said as Kendall was getting ready to go home.

"Everyone does." Kendall grinned. "As soon as I tell people where I work, they want to come see."

"Do you have a day you don't work after school?" Julian asked.

Alex nodded.

"Then please come by," Kendall said. "I'll give you

a tour."

"Thank you." Alex's eyes had been sad when Kendall first met her, but now they sparkled with excitement.

Mission accomplished.

"I need to get home to my dog." Kendall rose to her feet.

"I'll walk you out," Julian said. He led her to the door, his big hand on the small of her back.

Whenever he touched her that way, he never failed to make her feel delicate and important.

He stepped into the hall and shut the door behind them, pulling her into his arms and sealing his lips over hers. He kissed her, his tongue sliding inside. She moaned, threading her fingers into his hair and holding him tight, fully aware of every glide of his mouth over hers and the meeting of their tongues.

He pressed her against the wall, his body aligning with hers, his erection grinding against her stomach.

The sound of a door slamming penetrated her consciousness.

"Take it inside," a male voice said, sounding annoyed.

Kendall's cheeks heated as the neighbor walked by.

"Sorry," Julian muttered, one arm braced over her shoulder, against the wall behind her.

"Are you?" she asked, her body still buzzing from

that heated, sensual kiss.

"No." He grinned and brushed his lips over hers once more.

She laughed.

"I'll walk you down to get a taxi," he said, grabbing her ass for a quick squeeze.

She blushed and shot him a faux dirty look. And wondered when the last time was that she'd been this happy. The answer came to her immediately.

Never.

★   ★   ★

FOR SOMEONE WHO spent life spiraling between highs and lows, regular old everyday happiness was a scary thing to face. Kendall woke up in the mornings excited for the day but not soaring and in search of another, bigger high. In the normal scheme of things, she was working, planning for the future, and learning she could live a fulfilling life. Julian had added a dimension she hadn't considered, and she definitely spent a good amount of her therapy time discussing his return.

Her doctor, true to form, didn't offer an opinion one way or another, but asked probing questions that led her to look at all sides of her own behavior and choices, that she thought about as she spent the morning at work cleaning up the cages.

And there was a lot to clean. It seemed if one dog

got sick, another did, too, even if the illnesses were unrelated. The local vet who volunteered came by and checked everyone out, administering medication and fluids where needed.

She hadn't planned on a boyfriend. A man who was willing to integrate his life with hers, to accept her, flaws and all... just as she was accepting him. But for every minute of happiness, she had a few moments of *can this be real?* She realized that he'd contributed to that fear and the fact that she now trusted him scared her.

She washed her hands well with a lavender-scented antibacterial wash and returned to the front room to find Lauren Cantone talking to Josie.

"Lauren!" Kendall walked over, and Lauren gave her a hug.

"I told you I'd be by."

Kendall smiled. "I'm so glad you're here."

"Don't tell Brian. If he knew I didn't bring him along with me, he'd be so upset. But if I brought him, he'd fall in love, and be begging me to bring a dog home tonight."

"I totally understand."

"You aren't looking for a dog?" Josie asked from her seat at her desk.

"We were waiting until we sold our apartment, and this past weekend we got an offer and accepted! We also found a house we love. It's all moving so fast, but we've been ready for a long time." Excitement shone in her brown eyes. "I thought I'd come say hi to you and look at the dogs."

"My favorite thing." And at least it was all clean inside, Kendall thought wryly.

She took Lauren into the back, and they strode down the walk with the cages on either side. She stopped at each crate, paying attention to the individual dogs. Most were mixed breeds, some fluffy, others flat-haired, all sweet and looking for homes.

"As soon as we're in our new house, I'll bring Brian back," Lauren promised.

"Can I ask you something?"

"Sure." Lauren paused, leaning against the metal grating.

"You've known Julian for a while now. Nick said he's changed a lot in the last year, and I see it, too. But do you think it can last? That I can trust the man I see now?" Kendall bit the inside of her cheek.

On the one hand, it seemed like a betrayal to talk about Julian to his friend's wife. On the other hand, who knew him better than his sponsor's family? And ever since she'd considered confiding the truth to her sister about her relationship with Julian, one thing nagged at her. Trusting her own instincts. They'd betrayed her in the past. And it wasn't just her instincts involved now, it was her heart. Much more than before.

Lauren met her gaze. "You care about him a lot."

There was no point in denying it. "I do. And honestly he hurt me before. I'm afraid I'm listening to my heart too much." But her head was telling her she could believe in him, too.

"Here's what I know, from someone who's dealt with an addict their whole lives. The man you're seeing now, the sober, in control man who has learned his lessons, he's real."

"But he was sober when he hurt me last."

Lauren inclined her head. "I know. I think everyone's rock bottom is different. For some it happens when their family walks out and they realize they have to get sober because they've lost everything. For others it happens because they end up hurting someone else. A drunk driver can kill or injure someone in an accident."

Kendall winced at the realities and nodded her understanding.

Lauren went on. "In Julian's case, he held on to bad behaviors that probably preexisted the addiction. It took hurting and losing you for him to see who he'd become. He didn't like that man and he decided to change."

"Just because of me?" she asked.

"You were the catalyst that forced him to see himself." She shrugged. "Is it that simple? I guess in his case it was."

That, along with his life events that had shaped the man he was today, Kendall thought.

"Thank you, Lauren. I'm so glad you came by."

Lauren pulled her into a hug. "Me, too. Maybe we can get lunch one day?"

For other people, the offer might not mean much, but for Kendall, it meant she had something precious. It meant she had a friend.

Chapter Nine

OVER THE NEXT two weeks, Julian fell into a routine he could get used to. He woke early, worked from home as usual, then often met up with Kendall, spending his evenings at her apartment with the dogs until nearly midnight, at which point he headed home. He didn't want to leave Alex alone overnight.

In the time she had been staying with him, she'd been a model houseguest. She went to school in the morning and worked in the afternoons. Occasionally she made dinner for them both or accompanied him to Kendall's to eat. Or Kendall came up to his place and the three of them hung out for a while.

Julian admired how quickly and easily Kendall had taken to Alex, and vice versa. Kendall's new easygoing personality, her calm, caring demeanor had brought Alex out of her shell. It was obvious she hadn't had a mother figure in her life, and she looked up to Kendall.

On the nights he and Kendall were alone, they made the most of their time. There was plenty of talking and getting to know one another better, but there was also sex. Which was coming to feel like a lot more than just satisfying an itch with a woman he desired. It wasn't something he dwelled on, not when things were going so perfectly. He just wanted to indulge and enjoy.

Tonight he wasn't seeing Kendall, so he turned into bed early. He couldn't sleep, and it wasn't because Steve's body was aligned with his, pushing him to the edge of the bed.

Needing a distraction, he reached for his phone and called the one person who always made him smile.

His sister. "Hey squirt!" Julian said, pushing himself up in bed, resigned to a sleepless night.

"Hey, pain in my ass." Alyssa laughed.

"Is that any way to talk to your older brother?"

"It is when you haven't introduced me to your girlfriend… and you promised."

Julian groaned. "I know." He'd planned on broaching the subject soon… and then Alex had intruded. "We'll have to get you over here because I also want you to meet Alex in person."

"The girl who's living in your extra bedroom," Alyssa said, as if reminding herself.

"Right. She has nowhere to go."

"Aha, so you have two other women in your life. Should I be jealous?" Alyssa asked. Her quick chuckle told him she was anything but.

His sister was all sweetness and easygoing charm. She often spoke extra slowly, sometimes stuttered over a forgotten word or event, and needed the comfort of routine, but she was a genuinely kind, caring soul. How she'd ended up with Julian as a brother was beyond him. If she knew half the things he'd done...

"Julian, you aren't going to answer me? Maybe I should be worried." Alyssa's voice cut him off from giving himself a hard time.

"Sorry. I got lost in thought," he said honestly. "Of course you have nothing to worry about. You're my favorite squirt."

"So when can I meet them?" Alyssa asked.

"How about this weekend?" Julian made the offer hoping Kendall was free.

"Sunday," Alyssa said. "I work Saturday afternoon," she said slowly, as if she was thinking or checking her schedule.

"I'll check with Kendall and see what I can do," Julian said, pleased the two most important people in his life were finally going to meet.

★　★　★

KENDALL MET UP with Julian, Alex, and Julian's sister, Alyssa, at the dog park. The sun was shining overhead after a week of rain, and she welcomed the dose of vitamin D along with the warmth on her skin. Because it was early, the park was empty, but it would fill up soon enough because of the sunshine.

Waffles and Steve were excited to see each other and immediately began running, chasing each other in circles around the enclosed area.

Julian did the introductions, and Alyssa greeted Kendall with an excited hug. "It's so won… wonderful to fin…ally meet you!"

Kendall hugged her back, understanding her slower speech from Julian preparing her on the phone last night about the challenges Alyssa still faced from her traumatic brain injury. "I've heard a lot of good things about you," Kendall said to the pretty girl.

"Same here," Alyssa said.

"You look like your brother. Same eyes. Same mouth." Kendall grinned. "Good gene pool."

"Thank you."

Julian stood to the side, watching the interaction, a pleased smile on his face.

"Can I play with the dogs?" Alyssa asked, gesturing to where Alex was already kneeling down, petting Steve's belly.

"Of course. It's not comfortable on the ground. We can go back to my apartment, but it's such a beautiful day I thought it would be nice to hang outside for a little while."

"I love the fresh air." Alyssa smiled and walked a few steps and knelt beside Alex.

The two girls began to talk, their attention on the playful pups who alternated between nudging at their legs and going for each other.

"Want to sit?" Julian gestured to the bench they'd sat on the last time they were here together.

"Sure." She settled in beside him, their legs touching.

He reached out and curled his finger around a lock of her hair, tugging gently. "She likes you."

Kendall smiled. "We *just* met but I like her, too. She seems sweet."

"She is. The best kind of sweet. Innocent sweet."

She was sure all brothers wanted to think that of their sisters, but looking at how Alyssa interacted with Alex and the dogs, Kendall figured Julian was right. Alyssa was special.

After twenty minutes of watching the girls with the dogs, talking about everything and nothing, and the park filling with people and pets around them, an idea came to Kendall.

"Look at your sister."

Julian did as she asked.

"Look at how relaxed she is, the puppy in her lap and she's almost… serene."

"She is," he agreed. "She's like that when she's

working with flowers. It gives her peace."

"Did you ever think of getting her an emotional-support dog? Or letting her work with a dog to become one? It would be great for her to have a companion animal."

He scrubbed a hand over his light growth of beard, a sexy addition, in her opinion. One that made her female parts sit up and take notice. She'd like to feel that whisker burn between her thighs, she mused, trembling at the thought. But not in a public place, and that's where they were, so she waited for him to respond.

"I like the idea," he said at last.

"Does she have a doctor who would write a letter recommending she have an emotional-support dog for her condition?" Kendall asked.

Julian glanced over at his sister. "She does. What would she need it for?"

"Flying or if her landlord doesn't allow pets. But I think an animal would be a huge comfort to her," she said, just as Alyssa picked up Waffles and buried her face in the dog's fur.

"And I'm sold on the idea," Julian said, laughing.

His laugh hit all the right parts of her, emotionally and physically. He was so handsome in his aviators and bright smile, her heart squeezed at the sight of him, just as desire worked its way through her body.

"Thank you. The fact that you noticed that, it's going to make such a big difference in her life. I can just tell by looking at her." He stared at his sister with adoration and love, enabling Kendall to see just maybe why he'd gone to the lengths he had to ensure her well-being and future.

And a man who loved so completely, a man she was developing deep feelings for, couldn't be bad.

★　★　★

JULIAN WALKED INTO her apartment, Chinese food bag in hand, and she greeted him with a kiss on the mouth, one he'd been starving for all day. Her warm lips settled on his, causing his cock to do an eager jump.

A flying dog separated them when Waffles did a leap for the food, her paws landing on Julian's stomach. Steve, meanwhile, lunged for Waffles.

Julian raised the bag, keeping it out of the dogs' way. "Go play." He gestured inside and both dogs took off running. Of course, this was a New York City apartment and they couldn't go far.

"I was going to suggest we eat in the family room and relax, but I don't think the dogs will let us do either."

He laughed. "Kitchen table it is."

"Is Alex coming?" she asked.

He shook his head. "She has a test tomorrow. She's studying."

At the small kitchen table, he unpacked the boxes and she set down the plates and utensils. They shared pork dumplings, lo mein, egg rolls, spare ribs, and other traditional American-favorite Chinese foods.

"So... I was thinking," she said.

"About what?"

"My sister. I think you and I have been together long enough, tested the waters, so to speak. I've been considering telling her about us." She looked up at him with a serious expression on her face.

He dropped his chopsticks onto the table. "I'm sorry. Did you just say you want to tell your sister you're seeing *me*?"

"It's time I stand up for myself. She wants me to make my own decisions, to build my life. I'm doing that except she has no idea."

The muscles in his neck and shoulders tightened uncomfortably. "And how do you think she'll take the news? How do you think *Kade* will take the news?"

Kendall pushed herself up from her seat and walked around to his, settling herself onto his lap. "Not well," she said as she wrapped her arms around his neck, obviously trying to soften her words with her actions.

Still, it hurt to know he wouldn't make headway

with an apology or change of behavior with Kade. Julian had thrown away a friendship that meant the world to him, but he'd been in so much pain over his sister at the time, he couldn't see anything clearly. And later, he'd been a complete and utter bastard, jealousy and irrationality ruling his emotions. No excuses could be made.

"Hey." She clasped her hands on either side of his face. "What matters now is what we have. And I'll make them see that you've changed. Even if Kade won't come around, I just need to make sure my sister at least understands."

"The last thing I want to do is create a rift between you and your twin."

If that were true, you would have left her alone to begin with, his conscience mocked him. But he'd been incapable of keeping his distance, especially once he'd seen her again.

"Is understanding enough for you?" he couldn't help but ask. There was a big difference between her sister saying, *Okay, date the douchebag who hurt you,* and *Let's have Thanksgiving dinner together.*

All things he should have thought through before bringing her back into his life, for her sake. But as usual he'd been selfish, thinking of only his needs at the time.

She shrugged, which was as honest a response as

he was likely to get, and his stomach cramped at her having to make a choice between them. He hoped it wouldn't come to that.

"Let's not worry about it until it happens," she suggested. "I just wanted to give you a heads-up that I'm considering it." She threaded her fingers through his hair, in a blatant attempt to distract him, he was sure.

It was working. His thoughts shifted from their potential problems with her family to them, and she kept him too busy to think or worry until it was time for him to leave.

★ ★ ★

AFTER A LONG day of work, Julian took Steve out for a walk. With the sun overhead, white clouds dotting the sky, he enjoyed the time stretching his legs and being alone with his thoughts. He and Steve returned home after an hour. Because Kendall had a therapy appointment and he wasn't going to see her tonight, he planned on crashing early.

Except when he reached his floor, he found his door partially open and heard voices inside, which was unusual because Alex had never had company before. She said she had friends at school but always declined to bring them around. Given her foster care situation and the fact that she'd moved around, he wouldn't find it all that odd if she was lying and didn't have many friends at all. Hopefully time would change that.

Thanks to work and now Julian and Kendall, she kept plenty busy and out of trouble. As far as he could tell, she wasn't the kind of kid who caused problems anyway. From the time he'd met her as a young girl, she'd been easygoing and eager to please. She'd gotten along well with his sister, and because Alyssa was the type of person to embrace others, she called Alex to say hi on her own. Alex treated Alyssa well, not being put off by her speech or occasional forgetfulness.

So he didn't think there was anything really going on in his apartment, but he pushed the door open, wanting to see who was there without giving warning. Just in case.

Julian stepped inside, shocked to see Alex with her brother, Billy.

"Dude!" From his seat in the family room, Billy saw Julian first. His hair was cropped short, and he wore a pair of ripped jeans along with an old tee shirt.

A wariness prickled up Julian's spine as he bent to release Steve from his leash. Mixed emotions rushed through him, a combination of gratitude the man was no longer in prison and a guarded feeling of distrust. He couldn't put his finger on why, except Billy had always been one to make a side deal, to look out for number one. It made Julian uncomfortable that he was here now.

Had he just come to see his sister? Or did he want something more? Because for as long as Julian had known Billy, he'd had an angle.

"Hey!" Julian slapped his old friend on the back.

"Good to see you." Billy gestured to the table where an open beer can was beside an empty one. "Have a beer and we can catch up."

Julian's stomach cramped. Hell, he could be around alcohol no problem, but Julian didn't keep alcohol in the house, which meant Billy had brought the cans with him. He was drinking around his eighteen-year-old sister for no good reason. When the man was just out of jail. It didn't sit right with Julian.

He picked up the beer cans and headed for the kitchen, tossing one in the recycling container and pouring the other into the sink.

"Come on," Billy muttered. "That's good money down the drain," he complained. "Are you that much of a straight arrow now? I mean, Alex said you're clean now, but not even alcohol?"

"Not even that," Julian said, proud of himself and not about to let Billy make him feel bad about himself or the choices he'd learned to make.

"Umm, I'm going to get some homework done while you two talk." Alex ducked her head and escaped into the room she'd been staying in.

Julian had a hunch she felt bad he'd found her brother here, drinking, but he wasn't about to give her a hard time. He understood, at least from her perspective, the desire to see family and not to turn her brother away. Alex was just a kid. Billy was supposedly the adult. And the man was still a question mark as far as what he wanted.

"It's cool of you to take Alex in," Billy said, shoving his hands into his pants pockets.

Julian leaned against the kitchen cabinets, his arm on the Formica countertop. "She had nowhere to go. I wouldn't turn her out on the street."

"You're loyal. Always have been."

"Where are you staying?" Julian asked.

"At a halfway house for the next six months."

Julian did his best not to wince. It was Billy's life and he'd earned his way there. On the positive side, the man had somewhere to go and wouldn't be hitting Julian up for a place to stay. And there would be rules, restrictions, and people to watch him and keep him in line.

"I got a problem though," Billy said.

And now Julian knew why his sixth sense had been tingling. "What do you need?"

Billy ran a hand over his short hair. "Don't say it like that, man. I just owe some people some money. I was involved in some... deals on the inside and—"

"And you stiffed some people?" It wasn't a difficult guess that Billy had been out for Billy. Even inside prison walls.

"Something like that." He shrugged like it meant nothing. But if Billy owed people from prison, it wasn't *nothing*. "But if I don't pay back what I owe, they're going to come after me. And that's no way to start my life on the outside."

Julian rolled his eyes. "You don't think this is something you should have thought about before you worked an angle?"

Billy laughed. "Yeah, well, what fun is that if you aren't always pushing for more? But here's what I'm thinking." He kicked his sneakered foot against the floor.

"You're rich now. Everyone knows you hit those Blink guys up for big money. It was in the news. You can afford to help a brother out."

Julian pinched the bridge of his nose. "There is no money. I used it all to pay off debt from my sister's accident." And what was left he'd put into a trust for Alyssa, but that was none of Billy's business.

"You owe me," Billy said, his tone no longer light. "I took the fall—"

"That's bullshit and you know it. You were dealing. I agree I bought shit from you and they could have arrested me for possession if they'd caught me, but they didn't. No owing involved." Julian drew a calming breath. "As for money, you can't get blood from a stone. I don't have what I don't have."

But he wanted this man gone, so Julian pulled his wallet out of his pocket. "Here's a couple hundred bucks. I'll get you another grand but that's all I've got. And considering I'm taking care of your sister, I'd call us even." Julian did his best to hide his disgust.

He was looking after Alex because he wanted to help her, not because he owed Billy a damn thing. But the other man was too selfish to understand that. Clearly he didn't give a shit about his sister at all. And Julian wanted him out of his hair for good.

"Fine." Billy snatched the cash out of Julian's hand and had it pocketed before Julian could blink.

It was time to define terms. "*Fine* means fine for good. Don't come back asking for a handout, because after this, we're done." Julian spread his hands, indicating no more.

"Whatever," Billy muttered. "Just get the cash soon. I like my bones where they belong in my body."

What a fucking idiot, Julian thought. But what had he expected? That he'd changed? "You plan on hanging around your sister much?"

Billy clamped a hand around the back of his neck, rubbing it like he was stressed. "I'm not the fatherly type, but you never know."

Julian frowned. "So you came here for money, not to see her. Nice brother you turned out to be."

"Give me a fucking break." Billy scowled and stood up straighter. "I gotta go."

"Don't let me keep you," Julian muttered, knowing he would have to pick up the pieces for Alex when she realized her brother wasn't just a criminal but a selfish asshole, too.

But Julian preferred that to Billy being a permanent fixture around here, bringing around a bad crowd and exposing Alex to his bad influence. He'd just have to see if Billy became an issue or not.

"Don't forget my cash."

Julian headed for the door and held it open for his former friend. "Give me a day. I'll get you the money. How do I reach you?"

"I'll get in touch with you tomorrow."

"Fine." And then he never wanted to see Billy again.

Chapter Ten

THE NEXT DAY, Julian made a trip to the bank and withdrew one thousand dollars.

Cash.

He headed home and managed to work for a few hours before Billy called, voice raspy, obviously hungover, to demand they meet so he could get his money. Twenty minutes later, he'd paid Billy one grand, reminding him they were through for good.

But seeing Billy again had brought up all sorts of feelings Julian didn't want to have or experience ever again. Anxiety clawed at him, and though he didn't desire a fix, he wanted to avoid feeling like he wanted one. As a preemptive measure, Julian called Nick, and they met at an AA meeting.

An hour later, Julian had his head on straight and Billy in his rearview mirror, hopefully never to be seen or heard from again.

One night soon, he planned on taking Alex for dinner and having a conversation about the kind of person her brother was and what kind of influence he could be... if she wasn't careful and let him in should he decide to hang around. Hopefully without hurting her too badly.

"You okay?" Nick asked.

"Much better and I appreciate you coming out for an extra meeting this week."

A light breeze settled around them. The street was otherwise quiet.

"My pleasure. You know, I worry about moving out of the city," Nick said, stopping on the sidewalk so they could talk.

Julian shook his head. "Don't worry about me. I'll be fine. It's not like I won't know where or how to reach you. Besides, nights like this are rare."

"Right. It's not every day an old druggie friend shows up on your doorstep demanding money."

"This is true." He shoved his hands into his front pockets. "I paid him this morning while Alex was in school. He didn't mention her at all."

Given how Julian felt about his sister, the things he'd done to secure her future, the fact that Billy could walk away turned his stomach. At the same time, he was grateful and believed Alex would be safer without her brother in her life.

"Forget him. We both know she's better off in the long run."

"Right. Once the hurt and pain pass."

"Let's change the subject," Nick suggested.

"Sounds good to me."

"How about Kendall? Things are good?" Nick kicked at the ground beneath his feet. "I'm not one to gossip, but she seemed key to your happiness so I have to ask."

Julian burst out laughing. "You'll play matchmaker and try to set me up but you won't gossip?"

Nick merely grinned.

"Everything is great." Which meant he was nervous because nothing in his life stayed good for long.

He needed to see Kendall. Only she could calm his nerves. "I've got to go but thanks again," he said to his friend.

It was late but he didn't care. Inside him was a driving need to feel her soft body wrapped around his, to help calm the rapid beating of his heart and the fear that she might be taken away from him at any time.

The worry wasn't rational but it was real, at least in his mind. Witnessing the after-effects of his sister's injury, he'd taken drugs to numb the pain. His father had been long gone. Loss was real in his life, and Billy's reminder of his past had churned things up inside him. Yes, the meeting had helped, but he knew getting lost in Kendall would help more.

A short time later, he was knocking on her door. One look at her beautiful face and the panic inside him settled.

She wore a long nightshirt, her nipples hard and evident beneath the soft cotton, her bare legs peeking out from beneath the short hem.

"Julian! I wasn't expecting you." But she didn't look disappointed to see him. "Is everything okay?"

"I needed to see you," he said, stepping inside and shutting the door behind him. Waffles said her hello, and he paused for some petting time before rising to his feet.

Before Kendall could react, he swung her into his arms and strode for the bedroom.

"You like carrying me around," she said, winding her arms around his neck.

"I like *you*." He had a hunch it was more than that, but there was just so much his brain could handle tonight, and overthinking emotions wasn't on his agenda.

Her soft, curvy body molded against his, giving him strength and boosting his desire. Before he could set her onto the bed, she clasped her fingers together, preventing him from releasing her.

"Talk to me. What's got you so worked up?" she asked. "When I spoke to you this morning, you sounded preoccupied on the phone and didn't want to answer any questions."

He spun himself around and sat down, keeping her on his lap as he pushed them back against the pillows.

"I had a visitor last night. Alex's brother showed up, pretending to want to see his sister, but he really had his own agenda." No big surprise there.

He breathed in her sweet-scented hair and forced himself to continue. "He wanted money. And this morning I gave it to him because it was what was best for Alex. And for me if it meant he wouldn't come around anymore."

She leaned back, meeting his gaze, worry in her eyes. "What's to stop him from coming back and asking for more?"

Smart girl, he thought. He'd had the same concerns himself. He gave her the only answer he had.

"I'm not saying he won't be back. Just that he can't get what I don't have. Any settlement money was spent on bills and my sister, and the rest was put into a trust for her. End of money. End of story."

Kendall's eyes remained steady on his. "But seeing him has gotten you all worked up."

He nodded. "I went to an AA meeting to help take the edge off."

She nodded in understanding. "I guess that's the equivalent of me going to an additional therapy appointment during the week. Did it help?"

"It calmed the anxiety inside me, at least a little. Seeing Billy, dealing with him just brought my past too close."

She sighed and laid her head on his shoulder. "I'm sorry. I'm glad you came over."

"Me, too." He slid his hand beneath her nightshirt and up her back, stroking the soft skin, letting the circles he traced on her skin calm him.

"I have another way to calm you," she murmured, climbing off his lap.

Her hands went to his waistband, releasing the button on his jeans. "Stand up," she ordered. "And undress."

"Bossy." But he listened, toeing off his shoes, then unzipping and dropping his pants and the rest of his clothes, kicking them aside.

She dropped to her knees, leaned forward, and licked at the head of his cock, her small tongue causing a big reaction throughout his body. A tremor rocked him, only getting larger as she slid her mouth along his hard length, then pulled back, grazing her teeth lightly against his skin.

"Fuck." The word came out a groan as she licked and sucked, taking him deep into her warm, wet mouth.

She added a hand, cupping the base of his shaft and squeezing, as she pumped her hand back and forth, following along with her mouth. She moistened his dick, making for a smooth glide as she worked him over.

He groaned and grasped on to her head, threading his fingers through her hair and guiding her as he pumped into her, careful not to hurt her as he took the pleasure she offered.

He glanced down, meeting her wide gaze, her eyes glazed with desire, showing him she wanted this as much as he did. She picked up the pace, and he couldn't help but pump his hips along with her rapid motion.

A rush of desire washed over him; his balls drew up tight. He was going to come, and he didn't want it to be in her mouth. He pulled back, taking her by surprise.

"What's wrong?"

"When I come, it's going to be inside you."

Her eyes darkened with pleasure. "Oh yeah?" She rose to her feet and sat back on the bed, peeling her panties slowly down her legs.

Too slowly for his liking, and he yanked them down hard, need driving him.

She spread her legs, giving him a glimpse of her damp sex. He climbed over her and grazed his dick over her clit.

She whimpered at the soft contact. "I need you inside me now."

He wasn't about to argue. He arched his back, ready to thrust deep inside her when he remembered.

"Fuck. No condom. I didn't know I'd be coming here." He braced his arms on the bed, sweat trickling down his back.

"I don't keep them here anymore." She closed her eyes in frustration for a brief second before opening them and meeting his gaze. "I haven't been with anyone since you. And at my doctor's suggestion, I've had regular checkups. I'm okay… if you are. Plus I'm on the pill now." Pure need shone on her face, along with a hope and trust that was humbling.

"I haven't been with anyone, either. I swear." He'd been too devastated by his actions, by how he'd hurt her and what he'd done, to even think about dating another woman. Let alone having sex with one. "I'm clean. I promise you."

She blew out a long breath, her gaze holding his. "I want to feel you. Every bare inch."

He let out a low groan, raised himself over her, aligning his cock and gliding home. "Oh damn, baby, you feel good." Slick, soft, and cushioning him in warmth. He felt her everywhere, so different from when latex separated their bodies.

Nothing kept them apart now.

They moved as one, the sounds, the groans, the soft sighs all melded together as desire grew faster and more furious between them.

He pumped in and out, getting closer to Kendall

with each successive thrust.

He kissed her face, inhaled, breathing her in as she shook around him, her fingernails scoring his back, the pain mixing with pleasure as he climbed higher. Closer to climax.

"Julian, please," she panted in his ear. "So close. I'm so close."

He gritted his teeth, holding his climax, helping push her toward her own. He eased back, sliding his hand between them and pressing his finger against her slick clit.

"Oh God." She arched into him, and he pressed harder, moving his finger in small circles until she began to shake beneath him.

"That's it, I'm coming!" She cried out and he thrust deep, pounding into her until she stiffened and started to tremble once more.

Knowing she was coming again set off his own release, his climax detonating. He came, a mixture of physical release and intense emotions rocking him to his core.

★   ★   ★

KENDALL WOKE UP first, her skin wrapped in heat. Julian had pulled her into his arms, cocooning her with his big body. She sighed and snuggled back into him, still amazed he was back in her life.

Last night it had been evident he still struggled with his demons, but also that he was determined to fight them. AA was necessary to his well-being.

Apparently, so was she. She liked knowing when he was down, he came to her. And she felt bad for what he was going through. His past returning had to be tough.

She didn't want Billy around Julian any more than she wanted him around his sister. Kendall wasn't worried about drugs or Julian resorting to old ways. They'd come too far and she trusted him too much for that. But she was worried about how Billy's return affected and upset him.

She glanced at the clock on her nightstand, surprised it was after nine. They'd both overslept, which wasn't a problem for her. It was her day off. And she knew why she'd needed extra sleep, she thought with a grin. He'd kept her up last night with his hands all over her, doing amazing things to her body.

All the fear she'd had of their sex life changing, being less exciting because she was more mellow and calm, had been for nothing. Between the fun spanking the other night and the intensity of last night, she knew she had nothing to worry about. They were beyond compatible in bed.

And this time around, she'd learned they were also good for each other in other ways, as well.

She rolled out from under his arm, and he snagged her back, pulling her beneath him. "Going somewhere?"

"Nope." Not now that he was awake. "Are you feeling better this morning?" she asked, partly afraid she was doing the wrong thing by bringing it up again.

"Much better. But I feel bad that I left Alex. When I called last night, she said not to worry about it, but I don't want to make it a habit."

"I understand." She ran her fingers through his hair. "We'll just call it extenuating circumstances and leave it at that."

"I did tell her I wanted to have dinner with her tonight. I need to spell out the kind of man her brother really is. It tears me up inside to hurt her, but I want to protect her, too."

Her expression saddened. "That really is awful, but honestly she's better off. Would you like me to come along? Or would you rather be alone when you tell her?"

"I'll take all the support from you I can get." He leaned down and pressed his lips against hers.

She kissed him back, parting her lips and letting his tongue inside to tangle with hers. She felt the hard press of his erection against her stomach and was about to reach for him when the doorbell rang.

"Are you expecting someone?" he asked.

She wrinkled her nose. "No. Ignore them and maybe they'll go away." She kissed him again… and the doorbell rang again. Oh damn.

"Argh. Don't go anywhere." She jumped out of bed and pulled on a pair of sweats she'd left on the floor, grabbed a sweatshirt that was hanging on the chair by her vanity mirror, and rushed into the other room.

Just as she walked into the hallway, the door opened and her sister walked in, key in hand.

"Lexie! What are you doing here?" And how could Kendall get her to leave as soon as possible?

She panicked, knowing that though she wanted her sister to know she was seeing Julian, she didn't want her to walk in and be shocked by seeing him. But Lexie had let herself in using her old key. Which was now an emergency key. Which she'd never had a reason not to be able to use because if Kendall had a guy in her life, she'd tell her twin. And then her twin would know to use some discretion and not let herself into the apartment without warning. When not just any man but Julian was in her bedroom.

Yes, she wanted to tell her sister she and Julian were involved, but she'd wanted to talk to her, ease into the conversation. She'd planned on explaining how amazing Julian had been to her now, how much he'd changed, and what had prompted some of his behavior to begin with. And she could still handle it that way if Lexie left now, before she saw Julian.

"I'm sorry to just show up, but I knew it was your day off and how sometimes you sleep in. So I figured I'd just wake you with your favorite hazelnut coffee and muffins!" Lexie held up a bag with the logo from Kendall's favorite shop.

"Thank you," Kendall said, accepting the bag of her favorite food.

"I'll just put the coffee on the kitchen table and we can eat. And talk."

"But—"

Lexie turned toward the kitchen, but before she could take another step, Julian walked out of the bedroom.

"Is everything okay? Who was at the door?" He stepped out in his jeans, pulling his shirt over his head as he spoke.

Kendall closed her eyes as the inevitable unfolded.

"What in the ever-loving hell is *he* doing here?" Lexie yelled.

Kendall winced at her sister's sharp tone.

Julian stepped up beside Kendall. "I can explain."

Lexie frowned. "I don't want to hear anything you have to say." She turned to Kendall. "You, on the other hand, I want to hear everything. Talk to me. Are you off your meds?"

Hurt flowed through Kendall. "That's insulting." She'd come so far, for long enough now that her sister should have some faith. "I wanted to tell you, but I knew you'd react badly."

Lexie folded her arms across her chest. "Tell me what, exactly? That you're sleeping with him again? What's wrong? He didn't hurt you badly enough the first time? He didn't hurt Kade enough? You had to go back for seconds?"

Every word was a dagger to Kendall's heart. Her sister didn't know how she felt about Julian; she didn't understand the man he really was. And she clearly didn't give Kendall any credit whatsoever. Maybe she'd deserved that at one time, but she'd been proving herself over and over for almost a year. Longer than ever before.

Surely she'd earned some leeway in her choices. "Lexie, I'm sorry and if you give me a chance—"

"Not happening."

Kendall's stomach churned at the obstinate tone in her twin's voice. "Julian, let me talk to her alone." She rubbed her hands up and down her bare arms, chilled inside and out.

"I'm not leaving you to handle this alone." He stood beside her, determined and strong, and she appreciated the effort. But there was no way she'd get through to her sister if Julian didn't leave.

"Oh, because I'm going to hurt her?" Lexie asked, sarcasm dripping in her tone as she folded her arms across her chest in a direct replica of Kendall's.

"You already did hurt her. More than once in the last few minutes alone."

Kendall groaned. She didn't want these two going at it. It wouldn't accomplish a thing.

To her surprise, Lexie's angry face crumpled. "I shouldn't have asked if you were off your meds. But really, Kendall. Him?" She gestured to Julian. "What are you thinking? Or are you?"

Kendall put a hand on Julian's back. "Go, please. I'll call you later. I need time alone with Lexie."

"But—"

There was only one way to make her point, to Julian and to her sister. She stood on her tiptoes and pressed a reassuring kiss to his lips. "I'll be fine. I'll explain and I'll call you later."

"God." Lexie stormed off, headed toward the kitchen.

Julian grasped her shoulders, holding on tight. "Don't let her convince you I'm someone I'm not. Or someone I used to be. You know me," he said, the worry in his gaze making her realize she wasn't the only one feeling anxious.

If Lexie didn't come around, if she couldn't convince her sister to talk to Kade, the life Kendall wanted wouldn't exist. And she'd have to make choices she couldn't bear to make.

Chapter Eleven

THE COFFEE GREW cold as Kendall waited for her sister to calm down enough for her to explain how she'd ended up back in a relationship with Julian. Lexie paced the small area of Kendall's kitchen, muttering to them both. Kendall knew her twin well enough to know that until she got her frustration out, Kendall wouldn't be able to get a word in edgewise. Not one that would penetrate Lexie's brain, anyway.

"I don't understand. He broke your heart. He dug into Kade's past and brought out someone who accused him of date rape in college. All for money. How could you take him back?" Lexie finally turned to her and asked. "Make me understand."

Kendall took her sister's hand and led her out to the family room. "Let's sit."

Lexie chose the far end of the couch. "So I can see your face. I need to be objective and it's not easy." She twisted her hands in her lap and met Kendall's gaze.

She could only imagine what her sister was feeling, and knowing she had to go home and tell Kade... Kendall shuddered.

Kendall sat down, hands in her lap. "Julian adopted Steve," she said as her opening explanation.

Lexie blinked. "Seriously? He adopted a dog to get to you?"

"Owning a dog is a big responsibility. I'm pretty sure he must have wanted him," she said, not hiding her sarcasm. "But I'm not saying seeing me didn't factor into where he adopted from."

"I'm glad that cutie found a home. Go on."

"At first I refused to talk to him about anything other than the dogs. Then Steve got sick and he had no one with experience to call. The vet wasn't on call, so he contacted the shelter and I answered."

Lexie rolled her eyes. "And of course, soft-hearted Kendall had to help him in person."

"Yes." She stiffened at the implication that there was something wrong with doing the right thing. "The dog was sick, and I knew where to go and what to do. And then we started talking again. He apologized. From the heart and not just for hurting me but for what he did to Kade. He didn't offer up any excuses, either. He takes full responsibility and he regrets it, Lexie. He really does."

"It doesn't change anything," her sister said stubbornly. "What kind of person does those things?"

"The kind who was hurting and made mistakes." She'd come to understand Julian so much better, and it was up to her to get her sister to see the same.

"Hurt that he was left out of a big IPO because he was an addict?" Lexie asked.

Kendall blew out a deep breath. "Can you please lose the sarcasm?"

"Sorry."

Kendall had only one route possible to reach her twin. Although Julian's past wasn't her story to tell, without revealing the truth, her sister would have no reason to understand where he'd been coming from or what he'd endured.

"No, the kind of hurt that resulted from his sister being in a car accident when his mother was drunk driving. Back when they were in college, his mother was killed and his little sister had a traumatic brain injury."

Lexie's mouth opened wide. "I didn't know that. Does Kade?"

"Nobody knew. Julian bottled up his feelings, kept the facts to himself, and started doing drugs to numb the pain." Kendall ran her hand over her sweat pants, bunching the cotton and releasing it again in a nervous gesture.

"Why didn't he tell his friends?"

"I don't know. But his mother was an alcoholic, so addiction runs in his family. And his father was long gone by that time. His grandparents took over his sister's care and encouraged him to go back to school and graduate so someone could make money to help. Because, oh, did I mention his mother had let their health insurance lapse?"

"Oh my God."

"That's a lot of burden on a twenty-year-old, right?" Kendall asked.

"Yes. I get that. And I understand that's when he became an addict. But from what I was told, he was clean at the time he hooked up with you and when he did what he did to Kade. When he sued the guys for a piece of Blink." Lexie spread her hands wide. "So…"

"So he screwed up. He admits that. He was buried in debt, and he wanted his sister to have some kind of monetary cushion especially since she has residual issues. And he was so filled with self-hatred for walking away from the guys and Blink, losing out on the opportunity because he'd turned to addiction."

Kendall scooted closer to her sister and took her hands. "He never once used it as a reason. He said he won't ever try and use his past as an excuse for being a total asshole."

Her sister looked at her, helplessness in Lexie's gaze. "What changed then? What makes him a different man now?"

"He said he fell for me back then. And when he found out I was… am bipolar, that he'd used someone who had their own issues, who wasn't emotionally capable of dealing with what he'd done, he hated himself. He looked in the mirror and really saw himself for the first time. And he didn't like who he'd become."

When Lexie remained silent, Kendall went on. "He goes to AA meetings. Often. He has a sponsor and I've met him and his wife. They vouch for him, Lex. They see a difference in him. Please. Just open your mind toward him a little. Please." She held on to her sister's hand, begging for her life. Because being forced to choose between Julian and her twin just might kill her.

"Kendall..."

"Please? Just sit with this for a little while. Let it settle. Don't make any snap negative judgments."

Her sister pulled her hand back and rubbed her eyes. "You're killing me. And I have to tell Kade."

Kendall swallowed hard. "I know." She didn't expect Lexie to keep secrets from her husband. "I'm just hoping maybe with a little background and perspective, Kade can... I don't know. I'm not asking for him to accept Julian with open arms, but I'd like him to give Julian a chance, to see the man that I do now."

"This wasn't the fun breakfast I had in mind," Lexie muttered.

"I know."

"Do you? Do you have any idea the position I'm in?" She shook her head. "Never mind. I can't make any promises."

"I know." But she wasn't outright refusing to even consider the possibility that Julian had changed. That he had conquered his demons.

Lexie rose to her feet and Kendall pulled her into a hug. "Thank you."

Lexie hugged her back. "I love you, K."

Tears formed in Kendall's eyes, fighting past the lump in her throat, because she honestly had no idea how this all was going to end. "I love you, too."

Lexie stepped back. "I should get going."

"Okay." Kendall was disappointed.

She'd been hoping her sister would stay and at least eat the muffins she'd brought. Maybe then the hole in the pit of her stomach would disappear. But she'd dumped a lot on Lexie without any warning.

If her twin needed time, Kendall would give her time, but right now her main concern was Julian and making sure he knew everything was okay. She knew this was a conversation better had in person, but she also understood he was probably waiting to hear. She decided calling him made the most sense, would get the story to him the quickest.

She dialed his cell and he picked up immediately. "How'd it go?" he asked.

She blew out a deep breath. "About as you would expect. She was skeptical, especially at first, but I managed to calm her down and at least give her something to think about."

"How? What in the world could you have said that would convince her to at least consider giving me a chance?" he asked.

She lowered herself onto her bed and curled her legs beneath her. "Don't get mad, but I told her about your mother's accident and your sister." She held her breath, waiting in silence as he digested that nugget of information.

"It's not something I'm ashamed of. At the time I was embarrassed about my mother's addiction and behavior and wanted to numb the pain. I don't mind that you explained. I just don't think Lexie or Kade would buy it as an excuse."

"She wouldn't and I didn't try and sell it as one. Because you didn't explain it to me that way. I just wanted them to understand that things weren't as black and white as they might have seemed."

His harsh breathing sounded in her ear. "Are you okay?" she asked him.

"Not really. You?"

She shook her head despite knowing he couldn't see. "No." She was upset that her sister hadn't automatically trusted her judgment despite understanding why she couldn't. She knew Lexie's skepticism had more to do with Julian at this point than with Kendall herself. But it didn't make her feel any better.

"I'm sorry you had to go through that. I know how much you love your sister, how close you two are."

She swallowed hard. He could try to understand, but he couldn't possibly comprehend the duality of her emotions. First, there was the twin bond. Second, there was the fact that Lexie had been more of a mother to Kendall than her own parent had been. She'd looked out for Kendall when she'd been unable to take care of herself properly. She'd dropped plans and put her life on hold when Kendall wasn't properly medicated and her behavior was way too erratic.

As much as Kendall wanted to live for herself, she owed her sister a debt she could never repay. Mostly because Lexie had never once asked her to or made her feel as if she owed her. The last thing Kendall wanted to do was put a rift between Lexie and Kade or, worse, put Lexie in the dreaded position of having to choose between them. If anyone was going to make a choice, it would be Kendall. It was the least she could do.

"Kendall? I asked if I could see you this afternoon," Julian said, his voice low.

She sensed his pain, understood his feelings. She just couldn't bear his on top of her own right now. "I have things to do around here," she murmured. She needed time to think. "But I'll come by in time for dinner so we can talk to Alex together." As planned.

And a break would give them both much-needed time to digest the current situation—alone.

★ ★ ★

JULIAN TRIED TO lose himself in work, and he did manage to complete one project and begin another for a new client. Unfortunately he wasn't able to push the conversation with Kendall from his mind. How could he when she'd refused to see him?

He didn't doubt she had things to do on her day off, but he'd also heard the down tone in her voice. And though it matched his, she had much more at stake than he did in how her sister—and Kade—decided to handle Kendall and Julian's relationship.

The one thing he didn't want to do, the place he didn't want to reach, was one where Kendall felt like she had to choose between Julian and her twin. The Kade he'd known wasn't spiteful, but Julian had certainly backed him into a corner, and for all he knew, the man had changed. He had no reason to like Julian or to want him in his sister-in-law's life, no matter how much Kendall insisted he'd redeemed himself in some small way.

Over the course of the day, he decided the best

thing for him to do was to stay the course. Keep on working his way back to Kendall and hope that she had the strength to stick by him and her sister found it in her heart to give him a chance. And convince her husband to do the same.

★　★　★

KENDALL MET JULIAN and Alex at a pizza place near his apartment. They'd just finished sharing a pepperoni pizza and were waiting for the table to be cleared. Julian still hadn't broached the subject of Billy, and he was running out of time to do what he had to do. If he didn't talk soon, Kendall was going to have to start the conversation.

"So, you two have been acting differently," Alex said, taking Kendall by surprise.

She was quite perceptive for an eighteen-year-old, but Kendall didn't want her worrying about anything. "We're fine. It's just been a long day." Longer than the young girl knew.

Although Kendall doubted her sister was intentionally trying to torture her, she'd been tormented by Lexie's silence nonetheless.

"I wanted to talk to you about Billy," Julian said, changing the subject from them to Alex's brother.

"What about him?" Alex sipped on her soda, pulling in a long, loud slurp.

"I know he's your only family, but he's not the kind of guy you want to hang around too often," Julian said, obviously trying to be as delicate as possible.

"No kidding. He and his friends are dirtbags like the guys who stole my money." Alex scrolled around on the iPhone Julian had gotten her so she could keep in touch between school and work or if she had a problem.

Kendall choked on her own saliva. Okay, maybe Alex didn't need the speech to be careful about her sibling. But Julian was being careful.

"So I don't have to warn you to not get involved with any of his friends or his schemes?" Julian pushed on.

Alex placed her phone on the table and looked up, meeting Julian's gaze. "My brother's been an asshole since I've known him. Before he went in, I had a place to stay and that's it. And while he was in jail, I never heard from him except to tell me he was getting out. I don't expect anything from him. Never did."

Well, that was interesting, sad, and way too old a way of thinking for her age, Kendall thought sadly.

Julian eyed her warily. Kendall did the same. She wasn't going to let her get away with brushing off something so serious as her relationship with her brother. Whatever that might—or might not—be.

Alex needed to know she didn't have to keep her feelings bottled up inside and live with them eating away at her. "It's not easy to have a rift with a sibling," Kendall said.

And she ought to know.

Julian met her gaze, a mixture of wariness and sadness in his eyes. She hated what she was doing to him. She just didn't know how to fix it.

"It is what it is, at least in my case," Alex said, playing with the straw in her drink.

Kendall sighed. Either Alex was telling the truth and her brother's behavior and lack of caring really didn't bother her or she was hurting and damned good at covering it up.

"Well, I just want you to know," she said, reaching across the table and touching her hand, "I'm here for you. If you want girl talk or to talk about your family, school… anything… you can call me."

"Okay. Thanks," Alex said, her gaze already back on her phone.

Julian glanced at the waitress and gestured for a check.

"Actually can I meet you at home? I have homework to do," Alex said.

"Sure. Go ahead," Julian said.

Alex headed out, leaving Julian and Kendall alone. They hadn't seen each other all day, and they'd had a teenage buffer throughout the meal.

Now he studied her from across the table. "Are you okay?" he asked her.

"Yeah. It was just a tough day."

"Have you heard from your sister?" he asked, obviously wondering if Lexie had had a chance not only to digest the fact that her twin was dating Julian but to tell her husband.

"Not yet. But I did hear from Josie. Our sister shelter in Maryland got in a bunch of dogs. I didn't get the details, but we're going to bring some of them back to our shelter. She asked me to go down there for the weekend, deal with the paperwork, and accompany their person back here with the animals."

His eyes opened wide, his surprise evident. "You're leaving for the weekend?"

She nodded. "It's for work."

And it was good timing, she thought, feeling bad. But being away would give her time without the guilt about the time she spent with Julian, knowing her sister was upset. Or the time she spent away from Julian, knowing he was probably disappointed they couldn't be together. She was torn and frustrated. This trip came at just the right moment.

"I understand."

She wondered if he'd say more, but the waitress placed the check on the table, interrupting any serious conversation.

Julian picked it up and pulled bills out of his pocket, leaving the money on the table. "How about you come back to my place? We can relax and watch a movie."

She drew a deep breath, a sudden pain shooting through her chest. She could go and live with feeling torn and guilty or she could make it easy and give them the separation that would help her get her head on straight.

"I can't tonight."

"Can't? Won't? Or don't want to?" He leaned on the table and met her gaze.

She sighed. "A combination of each?" she said with regret.

She didn't want to set them up for a night of painfully looking at each other, knowing things were up in the air.

He clenched his jaw tight. "Well, at least you were honest." Even if he obviously didn't like what he was hearing.

"Julian, you can't possibly understand my relationship with my sister," she said, needing him to understand.

This situation wasn't just about her.

This wasn't about Julian and Kendall as a couple.

This was about an obligation Kendall had. A debt

to be repaid. And a desperate need Kendall carried for her twin to believe in her at last, to see that all the time she'd put into her, all the sacrifices she'd made, had been for something positive, real, and lasting.

"Then spell it out for me. I'm listening." He leveled his gaze on hers, both challenging and begging her to explain.

She clenched her fists beneath the table. "It's not just that we're twins, it's that she gave up her life for me for a very long time. To take care of me. To monitor my meds, my moods." She drew a deep breath. "Growing up, she left parties, lost guys she liked who didn't understand about me and didn't want to wait around for her. If I don't respect Lexie's feelings now, what does that say about me in return?"

He sighed, expelling a long breath. "I'm not going to tell you it's not gutting me, but I do understand." His eyes turned a deeper green and locked on hers.

"She's also pregnant."

He smiled. "And you don't want to upset her."

She reached for his hand, welcoming the contact, the warm embrace, the touch of his skin against hers. "I just want to hear back from Lexie. See if she's able to get Kade on board."

Neither one of them addressed the question that hung out there. What if Lexie and Kade didn't come to understand Kendall's relationship with Julian? What if her sister demanded she make a choice?

What would she do then?

★　★　★

KENDALL HEADED HOME, and Julian grabbed a cab for himself and headed directly for Nick's, showing up uninvited on his best friend's doorstep. He wasn't ready to go home and be alone, and his friend always had words of wisdom. He needed that now, more than ever.

He banged on the door until Lauren answered.

"Julian! Is everything okay?" she asked, gesturing for him to enter.

"I'm really sorry to just show up, but I needed to talk."

She pulled her lip between her teeth. "I'm sorry, but Nick is out showing some apartments to people who couldn't go until after work. He should be home soon though. Want to come in for coffee?" she offered.

He smiled in gratitude and followed her inside. "Where is Brian?" he asked, glancing around as they walked to the kitchen.

"Sleeping at a friend's."

She paused at the single-cup coffeemaker and turned on the machine. While she made them coffee, his with a drop of milk and hers, he noted, she heavily added cream and sugar to, they talked about this and that, until she joined him at the table.

He wrapped his hand around the warm mug of coffee and took a long sip. "Thank you," he said.

"You're welcome." She smiled.

"So I hear congratulations are in order. You sold this place?"

She nodded, eyes filled with happiness. "I can't believe how fast everything's moving. We went to contract already. Closing is in two months. And we found the most amazing house in Westchester."

"When it's meant to be, it's meant to be."

"It's too bad you're not in the market, because there's another house for sale on the same street." She glanced at him over her coffee mug.

He laughed. "As amazing as that sounds, I think a house would be lonely with just me rambling around."

"You have Steve, and he'd have a yard." She shrugged. "You never know. Your life could change in an instant. Mine did." She waggled her eyebrows at him, giving him no doubt she was talking about him and Kendall.

"No rushing my relationship, Lauren," he said lightly.

Although he couldn't say he hated the idea of living in the suburbs, having a deck on which to barbeque and a backyard.

And a woman to share it with? If that woman was Kendall, a voice in his head answered. Who'd have thought Julian Dane would yearn for the house and the white picket fence?

He blew out a long breath, knowing at this point he was far from being able to consider even asking Kendall to go to dinner, let alone anything more serious. After all, wasn't that why he was here? To talk to Nick about his problems?

He and Lauren chatted a little about Brian and his having to switch schools when September rolled around, and how she couldn't wait to bring him to the shelter for a dog when the move was complete.

Finally Julian heard the sound of keys in the lock and the slam of the door.

"Looks like I should make another cup of coffee," she said, greeting her husband as he walked into the small room.

"No coffee for me," Nick said, then turned to Julian. "This is a surprise. Everything okay?"

"Yes. I just… Hell." Now that Nick was here and Julian had had a chance to calm down, he felt like an idiot for just showing up.

"Julian needs to talk, and I'm going to take a long, luxurious bath." Lauren poured what was left of her coffee into the sink. "It was good catching up," she said to Julian.

She paused to kiss Nick. "See you in a bit."

Nick eased himself into the seat across from Julian. "You've had a long day. Sorry to just show up here," Julian said.

"Actually I didn't work this afternoon, just tonight, so no worries. What gives?" Nick asked, always agreeable, always there when Julian needed him.

He hoped he gave the man at least half the friendship Nick gave him.

Since Nick knew his history with Kade, Lexie, and Kendall, the summary was pretty quick. "I slept at Kendall's last night. Her sister walked in on us this morning."

Nick winced. "I take it she wasn't happy to find you there?"

"Understatement." Julian leaned back in his seat and folded his arms across his chest.

He went on to explain Lexie's negative view on them as a couple, and how he and Kendall had left things between them tonight. "She's going away for the weekend and wouldn't come over. She's torn in two and it's killing me to see. I hate that it's my fault."

Not to mention her words, which were still running around his head. *I just want to hear back from Lexie. See if she's able to get Kade on board.*

What if she couldn't?

Julian had known better than to ask. "I feel like my

entire life can be decided by a man who rightfully hates my guts." He ran a hand through his hair in frustration.

"Your entire life, hmm?" Nick leaned an arm on the table. "A man only makes an extreme statement like that if he's all in with a woman."

"All in? Of course I'm all in. I love—" He reared back in his seat, shocked the word had come out of his mouth, even if he wasn't completely floored by the emotion.

He'd known for a while he was falling hard for Kendall, but admitting that he loved her out loud for the first time had taken him off guard.

Nick grinned. "Exactly. You love her."

"I damn well do." And it would rip him apart if Kendall didn't feel the same way, or if she decided her sister's and Kade's feelings meant more than his. Than her own.

He loved Kendall Parker, and Nick gave him time to digest the information.

Love was a new emotion for Julian. Oh, he loved his sister, but he'd never had that depth of feeling for a woman before. He'd never wanted someone's happiness more than his own. Not Mr. Julian Self-Serving Dane.

Everything about Kendall was different. It wasn't just that their physical compatibility was off the charts, but now that they'd spent real, quality time together, there was so much more to their relationship than sex. Kendall was sweet and compassionate, as evidenced by her feelings for the dogs in her care and how she'd instinctively reached out to Alex with the offer to turn to her for anything.

Kendall had known, just as Julian had, that Alex was no doubt covering up her feelings about her neglectful brother. Kendall had also related to Alex's situation because she was struggling to keep her relationship with her twin from falling apart. Another quality Julian admired about her.

Kendall was loyal, and he hoped her sister appreciated just how much she was willing to sacrifice. And she was emotionally strong. Even if she didn't comprehend that, Julian saw all she'd been through and overcome without bitterness or anger.

She had attributes he wanted in a partner, even if he hadn't known he was looking for one. And apparently, just as he figured it out, he was in jeopardy of losing her.

"Maybe it's Karma reaching out to bite me in the ass," Julian muttered. "I used her, hurt her, and now that I can't live without her, I might just have to." His chest contracted painfully.

Nick eyed him seriously. "The solution seems obvious to me. Are you going to sit around and let fate and Kade Barnes dictate what happens in your life?"

Julian blinked at his friend's blunt, astute comment. Just like that, the solution came to him, bursting through his brain.

"Like hell I am." Looked like it was time for him to pay his one-time friend a visit and have his say.

Chapter Twelve

E ARLY THE NEXT morning, while Kendall was on her way to Maryland, Julian walked into the chrome-accented office space of Blink, located in a renovated garage in Soho. Just as he'd expected, his arrival made waves because he'd shown up here before—during his asshole days—and people knew Kade didn't want anything to do with him.

Whispers and stares greeted him as he walked across the open floor plan. He did his best to ignore them and headed for where he saw Lexie standing. As she was her husband's personal assistant, Julian wasn't shocked when he had to get past her to see his one-time friend.

He strode up to the desk where Lexie stood, arms folded across her chest. For all that she and Kendall were twins, Julian would know his girl in a heartbeat. The woman dressed in a pencil skirt and white blouse, giving him the wary eye, wasn't her.

Lexie rose to her feet, rocking back on her heels. "Well, this is a surprise."

"I can't imagine it is," he said calmly but firmly.

"Do you really think I'm going to let Kendall fight my battles for me? I'd like to see Kade. Please."

A flicker of something lit her gaze. Admiration or respect were probably too strong, but on some level, he'd shocked her.

"You're going to stress him out," she said, concerned for her husband and the anxiety they both knew would be triggered by this confrontation.

"Probably," he agreed.

She frowned at that. "My sister must have strong feelings for you or else she wouldn't put all of us in this position."

Julian hoped Kendall loved him, too. But that wasn't something he planned on mentioning to her twin before he'd ever had a chance to tell Kendall.

"Are you going to announce me?" he asked with a raised brow. "Or do I get the honor of surprising Kade?"

She narrowed her gaze and blew out a long breath. "I'll be right back." She walked into her husband's office, closing the door behind her.

He glanced around, relieved neither Derek nor Lucas seemed to be at the office. Assistants huddled around their desks chatting and whispering, but no sign of the other co-founders. He was grateful for the reprieve. Julian would rather deal with one old pal at a time.

He'd have his hands full enough with Kade. Back in college, Julian had been closest with him, which was why the rift was probably the greatest between them now. But it was past time to make amends, not only because of his feelings for Kendall but because he was genuinely sorry for putting Kade through the shit he had. He'd had an immediate bond with Kade, and in retrospect, Julian should have gone to him with his problems. Life would have been a hell of a lot different if he had. But if there was one thing AA had taught him, it was that there was no looking back. Only apologizing, learning, and going forward.

A few short minutes later, which felt more like an uncomfortable hour, Lexie stepped out and motioned for him to join her. "Come on in."

He stepped toward her. "I don't mean anyone any harm, Lexie." He wanted Kendall's sister and Kade's wife to understand this wasn't a game to him. This was his life, too.

She grasped his arm in a desperate grip. "I hope you mean that, because you're talking about the two most important people in my life."

He believed her. He just wasn't sure she gave Kendall, the new Kendall, enough credit. "If you love your sister as much as you claim, you'll start to trust her judgment and let her make her own decisions." And on that note, he passed her by and walked into

Kade's office.

He came face-to-face with his old friend. Dressed in a pair of faded jeans and an old light blue tee shirt, Kade stood by his aluminum desk, rubbing the face of his watch with his thumb. A soothing gesture to his OCD. Kade had always found those.

"Ever since I heard the news that Lexie found you with Kendall, I wondered if you'd have the balls to show up here," Kade said by way of opening their conversation.

Julian shook his head at the man's insinuation. He'd been a lot of things. He never wanted to be a coward.

He met Kade's hostile gaze head on and offered up the one thing he'd never given him. "I'm sorry."

There weren't two words more difficult to say.

Kade ran a hand over his short hair, eyeing Julian warily. "Lexie told me about your mother's accident, your sister's injury."

Leave it to Kade to go right for the kill.

"What the fuck, Julian? Why didn't you just tell me? Or any one of us? You know damn well we would have been there for you, no questions asked. No judgment given."

Julian swallowed hard. It was easy to look back and think what he should have done. Back in the day, he could have turned to Kade, Derek, or Lucas. Instead he'd chosen to go it alone.

He'd also had his reasons. "I'm not saying your life was easy, but you had a father who'd do anything to make sure you succeeded. Who stood by you, even if you didn't like his methods," he reminded his old friend.

Hell, Kade's father had paid for a cover-up of a date rape accusation for a crime that his son hadn't even committed, just to be safe.

"I, on the other hand, had a mother whose poor choices and lack of caring led to her death and my sister's traumatic brain injury." There couldn't be a starker difference between their families. "And you can't understand why I was too embarrassed to share? Or why I turned to drugs to make me forget?"

Kade leaned a hip against the desk, no judgment in his gaze. Just a cool detachment that hurt.

"I can understand your reasons. Doesn't mean I have to like them. Tragedy happens. But it's not an excuse for what you did to me, to the guys, and to Kendall."

On that they agreed. "No, it's not. And if you'd let me finish, you'd know that's exactly how I feel."

Kade jerked his head up.

"I'm an addict," he admitted, the words difficult to say but necessary to his continued recovery. And though he normally accepted the label, today it hurt like hell to bare his soul.

"I'm in recovery," he went on. "And have been for a long time. I've come to terms with the things I did, and I regret them. I don't make excuses. So I'm here to say I'm sorry for everything I did. From bailing on Blink to the dirty, underhanded tactics I used against you. And most of all, for hurting Kendall." He shoved his hands into his pockets and rocked on his feet.

Waiting as silence fell between them and Kade digested Julian's words.

"Okay. Let's say I believe you mean those things," Kade said cautiously. "Apologies and regrets don't make you the right person for Kendall."

Julian shook his head. "And you think it's fair that somehow you've become the judge and jury of who she sees and what makes her happy?" There was an arrogance there he didn't see a reason to point out right now. "Kendall feels like she owes Lexie, and she wants her sister's approval so badly she'll give up her own happiness to ensure she doesn't hurt or disappoint her. How is that fair to Kendall?"

Kade pushed himself off the desk and strode toward the big window behind him. He stared out at the city, as if looking for answers.

"Look, I'm not asking for your forgiveness or your friendship." Okay that was a lie, Julian thought, because he would embrace both. He just knew better than to believe either could ever happen. "I'm just asking that you don't pressure Kendall. Let her make her own choices and trust the decisions she makes."

"And leave it to you to fuck it up on your own?" Kade asked. "I can do that."

Asshole. Julian straightened his shoulders defensively. "I just might surprise you," he muttered. "And I hear congratulations are in order. I wish you and Lexie all the best," he said, forcing out the words that he meant, even if Kade's attitude bugged him.

"Thank you."

Julian turned and walked out the door.

His heart pounded hard in his chest, the emotions flowing through him too many and varied to name or parse out. A part of him understood Kade's honest skepticism, but dammit, would a break be too much to ask for?

Apparently so.

As long as he and Lexie gave Kendall the space to decide what she wanted, Julian considered it a win. He'd given Kade something to think about. That was all he could do for now.

As for himself, he'd just have to prove Kade wrong and show the other man how much he cared for Kendall. That this time he wasn't out to hurt her.

★ ★ ★

KENDALL MIGHT HAVE been grateful for the chance to get away, but she missed Julian. She missed the easy give-and-take between them. She'd loved spending her evenings with him and sometimes Alex. There'd been no pressure between them. No worry about what the other person was thinking. She didn't have to worry about whether or not he'd call.

He always did.

They automatically knew they'd pick an apartment and be together in the evenings, unless she had therapy or he had AA or an appointment.

She'd ruined that.

She hadn't gone home with him after dinner with Alex, and he'd taken that to mean she needed space. She'd told him she was leaving for Maryland in the morning, and she hadn't heard from him. Not a phone call or a text.

What did she expect? By changing their routine, by rejecting his offer to come over, hadn't she all but asked for that space? She had. And she didn't like it one bit. Nor did she reach out, because she just didn't know what to say.

At their sister shelter, she found a group of dogs that had been kept in an elderly woman's apartment. She'd hoarded the dogs, then passed away. They'd come into the shelter dirty, matted, hungry, sad, and pathetic.

They'd since been groomed and checked out by a vet, and there were so many it broke her heart. But in this group, she saw potential. Friendly dogs, loving animals who just wanted to please. She'd keep an eye on a few and maybe be able to suggest them for Lauren and Brian, and one in particular for Alyssa. Time would tell if they got along with other animals, if they were good with children, if they could be trained into an easygoing emotional-support dog.

She'd love to share all this news with Julian, but she couldn't. And not because he wasn't reaching out on his own. No, she couldn't tell him because it wasn't fair to get his hopes up that they could return to their old relationship if she was just going to have to walk away, breaking both their hearts.

So she pushed her own wants aside and dove into work at the Maryland shelter for the weekend, sticking to her personal vow of radio silence.

Until she could figure out how Lexie and Kade felt. And what she wanted and needed to do.

★　★　★

JULIAN BURIED HIMSELF in work. He set up calls with people who wanted to hire him and continued work with existing clients. If he didn't have a personal life, he could damn well focus on his business. The only drawback to the productive weekend was a persistent visitor.

Billy.

For a guy who wasn't very brotherly, in his own words, he sure as hell seemed to want to be with his sister. On Friday night, Alex was home and Julian had no choice but to let Billy in. He hung out for an hour, and Julian refused to leave him alone with Alex, which, he could tell, annoyed the other man to no end.

Julian didn't care. He couldn't shake the feeling that Billy wanted something more... and he was determined to make sure he didn't get it.

On Saturday, Billy returned. From his clear displeasure when Julian opened the door, he obviously didn't realize Julian worked out of the house and would always be home.

He arrived with his eyes bloodshot and bleary. He was hungover and not a sight he would want Alex to see.

"Where's my sister?" he asked, leaning against the frame.

"Working. You know, at a job?" Julian asked with sarcasm. Something Billy knew nothing about. He doubted the other man would try to find decent employment no matter what the court system dictated.

Billy frowned. "Where's she work?"

That was on a need-to-know basis, and Billy didn't need to know. "She doesn't need to be disturbed at work. If she wants you to know, she'll tell you." Julian kept a hand on the partially open door.

Billy shoved a sneakered foot in the door. "You can't keep my sister from me."

"I'm not. She's not here. And you said you weren't the brotherly type, so what gives? Why the hell are you hanging around?" Julian asked.

"None of your damn business." Billy spun and walked away, and Julian did what he'd been itching to do since he'd opened the door.

Slammed it closed.

Saturday night Julian took Alex out for dinner. She'd sensed his bad mood, and he'd already told her Kendall was away working this weekend, so she was smart enough not to bring up the subject again. He convinced her they should put their phones away so they could talk over their meal. Better for him because he obviously wasn't going to hear from Kendall while she was gone and he needed a distraction.

After they finished dinner at a Mexican restaurant, Julian decided to broach a subject he wasn't sure Alex had given any consideration.

"So have you thought about college?" He caught her mid-sip of soda, and she choked on the liquid. "Sorry. You okay?" he asked.

She nodded, her eyes watering a little. "Yes. And to answer your question, I decided there was no way I could afford it."

She didn't meet his gaze, and his heart squeezed tight in his chest. "What if you could? What if I helped you?"

He'd given this a lot of thought, and his business was flourishing. High-six-figure flourishing. He didn't have that many expenses now that Alyssa was funded by the trust.

When he'd mentioned it to Alyssa, which he'd done because he didn't want his sister to find out and be upset she wasn't told, Alyssa had been excited for Alex. She'd also insisted they dip into the trust because there was money there that Julian had allocated for college, that Alyssa hadn't used.

Julian hadn't made any decisions about going that route.

And he wanted to give this sweet girl a good start in life. God knew, she'd come out of a rough situation with more grace than many people would have managed to have. He admired her.

"I couldn't."

But in her wide eyes, he saw something he hadn't noticed there since he'd met up with her on the street.

Hope.

"But I can and I'm offering." He reached out and clasped her cold hand.

"Why?" she asked.

That was an easy answer. "Because I couldn't do it for my sister. The accident changed the course of her life. Let me do this for you. An education is important to whatever you want to do in life." And he wanted to get her away from lowlives like her brother.

She sniffed and grabbed a napkin, wiping her eyes. "I don't understand why you're so good to me."

"I feel … like I should have done more for you when Billy went to jail. That if I was clean at the time, and hadn't been so selfish, I'd have offered to help you out anyway. You could have avoided foster care. So please let me do this. You'll be helping me, too." He'd feel less guilty for abandoning her to the system.

She jumped up, came around to his side of the table, and hugged him tight. "Thank you. Just … thank you."

He grinned, his throat full. "You're welcome." He felt damned good about how this conversation had gone.

Even if his love life was in the toilet, he'd just changed the course of Alex's life. And about that, he could feel proud.

★ ★ ★

SUNDAY MORNING, JULIAN took Steve for a long walk, and when he returned, Billy was just leaving, walking out the front door of the building. He didn't stop to talk, meeting up with a group of dirty-looking guys on the corner.

He rushed upstairs and let himself inside to find Alex standing in the hallway, looking shaken and upset.

He unhooked the dog's leash, and Steve ran for his water bowl.

Julian grasped Alex's elbow and led her to the couch, where he sat down, pulling her beside him. "What's wrong?"

If Billy had said or done anything to upset her, Julian would strangle him.

"I can't say." She attempted to stand, but he called her name.

"Alex, wait. What did you Billy do to upset you?"

She bit down on her lip so hard she drew blood.

He clenched his hands into fists. "Alex?

A sob escaped her throat. "He wants me to sell drugs. To find kids who want some and send them to him. He'd be their dealer."

Her voice cracked, and it took all of Julian's self-control not to lose it in front of the upset girl.

He blew out a long breath and sighed. "What did you tell him?"

She shook as she answered. "To go away and leave me alone. But he said I owed him. That he gave me a place to sleep and paid for my food when I was younger and now it was time for payback." Tears dripped down her face.

Anger, real, genuine anger filled Julian. "Did he say where to send these kids?" Julian asked. "Did he give you an address?"

She nodded and spouted the information.

The vise in Julian's chest eased a little. "I'll take care of it," he said through gritted teeth.

"What are you going to do?" she asked, wide-eyed and panicked.

He let out a low, ugly laugh. Not what he wanted to, which was to beat the other man senseless.

"I'm going to do some digging." He hadn't become a computer genius without picking up some skills. "I'll find out who Billy's parole officer is and let them know where they can find him during his daylight hours. With a little luck, he'll land himself back in jail in no time"

He glanced at Alex, worried she'd be upset he was plotting to send her brother back to jail. Regardless of what Billy had asked of her, they were blood related.

But she merely looked relieved.

"Meanwhile, you send him to me if you have another problem. Okay?" he asked.

"Okay," she whispered.

★ ★ ★

KENDALL CAME HOME Sunday afternoon and worked with Josie and the Maryland employee to get the dogs settled in their new pens. It always broke her heart, to move dogs from place to place and note their confusion and sad little faces. If she had her way, she'd live in a house with acreage and the ability to take in more than one dog.

Of course, she was afraid she'd become the old dog lady with more dogs than friends. But that wasn't something she would dwell on.

She was so tired she slept from eleven p.m. on Sunday to eleven a.m. on Monday, as Josie had given her the day off for a job well done. She woke up more rested.

Still not happy.

Still missing Julian.

Still growing more and more annoyed with the silence from her sister and Kade. She planned to corner them both at Blink this afternoon and hear what they had to say. Only then could she begin to make her own choices and decide what to do with Julian.

God, it hurt to even think about breaking things off with him. But she couldn't imagine not having her sister in her life, either.

"I can't think about this until I know more." She dressed, grabbed Waffles, who was always welcome at Blink, and took a taxi downtown.

She showed up to find Lexie in Kade's office, the door open, so she knocked and walked in.

"Hi," she said to them both.

"Kendall! I was going to call you after work. Hey, Waffles," Lexie said, bending down and beckoning to the dog.

Kendall released the leash, and Waffles ran for her cuddles.

"Hi, Kendall," Kade said in his deep voice.

"Hi."

"How was Maryland?" Lexie asked, rising from her crouching position.

"Fine. And I don't want to talk about Maryland or dogs or anything else that's trivial. You two have my life in your hands, and I haven't heard from either of you. Now—"

"Kendall, let's sit," Kade said in a tone that worried her.

"Let's just talk right now." She folded her arms across her chest. "I understand that you have hard feelings with Julian, that you're angry, that you don't trust him, and that you have good reason. But I do." She placed her hands near her heart. "He's proven himself to me over and over again. All I'm asking is that you give him a chance. Or give me a chance to prove that he's changed."

Kade glanced at Lexie. "I say we tell her now."

Lexie's face crumbled and tears filled her eyes. "I wanted to wait. I wanted more time…"

Nausea filled Kendall. "What's going on?"

"Honey, let's sit," Kade said. He led her to the sofa in the back of his office and they settled in, her heart pounding hard in her chest.

Lexie sat in a chair across from them.

"You're scaring me."

Kade took her hand. "Right after Lexie told me she walked in on you and Julian, I hired a private investigator to tail him and see what he was up to."

Kendall blinked, barely believing what she was hearing. "You what?"

"Hired a PI."

"I heard you. I just can't believe you did that. It's such a violation of privacy. It shows such incredible disrespect for me—" She jerked her hand back, out of his grasp.

"Kendall, it's just the opposite," Lexie said, siding with Kade.

"You knew." Pain shot through her. "You knew and you didn't tell me. You let him spy on Julian. I can't believe this!" She jumped up from her seat.

"Kendall, you need to hear what we found out. It took one short weekend for him to come up with something," Lexie said, standing and coming to her side.

Kendall narrowed her gaze. She'd been away this weekend, but she couldn't imagine what they'd discovered that would change how she felt about Julian.

"What? Tell me."

Kade rose slowly, his gaze on hers. "He's got an ex-con, ex-drug dealer coming in and out of his apartment. All weekend. His friends were hanging around outside and they aren't any better than he is."

Billy, Kendall immediately thought. The man the PI saw had to be Alex's brother. The joke was on Kade and Lexie, but she wasn't about to enlighten them.

"That's it? That's what you've got?"

"Isn't it enough?" Lexie asked, sounding horrified. "He's hanging around with a known drug dealer, and Julian is an addict, Kendall. An addict. What do you think this means?"

Of course they'd think the worst. Kendall did wonder why Billy was still coming around after he'd been paid off, but she was sure Julian had a good explanation.

Her sister and her husband, however, had betrayed her faith by hiring someone instead of trusting Kendall's words and her judgment.

"You had no right," she said, her voice rising.

Waffles barked at her obvious upset.

"Shh," she said, gesturing for her to come. She

petted the dog's soft fur, feeling better herself.

"Kendall, we love you. We want what's best for you. And if that means looking out for you in ways that you might not like, so be it," Kade said.

"I disagree." Kendall re-hooked Waffles' leash without meeting Kade's gaze. "I asked you to do something for me. To take my word for a man I've come to know very well. And you went behind my back and had him investigated."

"Kendall—" Lexie said.

"I'm leaving." She curled her hand around Waffles' leash. "And don't make me choose between you and Julian," she said, realizing that's what she'd been doing since Lexie found out. Pushing Julian away. "Because you might not like the result."

Chapter Thirteen

J ULIAN WASHED STEVE'S dish and poured him fresh water, something he felt like he was doing constantly, rising and adding water to the bowl. His doorbell rang, taking him by surprise. He wasn't expecting company, and since summer had started and school ended, Alex was at work at the library.

He hoped it wasn't Billy. He wasn't in the mood to deal with him right now. Julian had managed to track down his parole officer and give him the information he needed to know about the activities Billy was engaging in and what he'd asked of his sister. The rest was in their hands.

If Billy showed up here again, Julian would make it clear the cops would be waiting if he tried to contact his sister in the future.

He glanced through the peephole, shocked to see Kendall standing there. She wore a pretty summer dress and sandals, but her expression was serious and she didn't look happy.

His pulse ratcheted up a notch as he opened the door and they came face-to-face.

"Hi." She bit down on her lower lip, sounding hesitant.

"Hi."

"Can we talk?" she asked.

He nodded. "Come on in."

She stepped inside as Steve barreled toward her, excited to see her after so long. She took the time to give him the loving attention the dog desired, and he knew how pathetic it was that he was jealous of an animal.

He closed the door behind them. "Let's go into the family room. Alex is at the library." So they were alone.

"How was your trip?" he asked after they'd chosen their seats, apart from each other.

It fucking killed him that they'd come to this, because of his past and nothing that he or she had done now.

She wrung her hands, then picked up a tech magazine he'd left on the table in front of the sofa, then placed it back down. "My weekend in Maryland with the dogs was productive. The poor things. They showed me pictures and some were in such bad shape. But they're good now."

She smiled but it seemed brittle, as if she was as uncomfortable as he felt at the moment. "But I don't want to talk about work. I just came from Kade and

Lexie's—well, I dropped Waffles off at home first instead of dragging her all over Manhattan—and… God, I don't even know where to begin."

"Was your talk with Kade about my visit?" he asked. Because he could only imagine what Kade had to say about their encounter at his office last week.

She blinked in surprise. "You went to see him?"

Julian rose and walked around the room, pacing because he couldn't sit still. "I guess he didn't think it was important enough to mention to you."

"No, he had other things on his mind," she said bitterly. "Like the fact that he hired a private investigator to watch you."

Julian spun around. "Excuse me?" So that's how Kade opted to mind his own business and let Julian *screw things up on his own?*

She looked away, as if embarrassed and unable to meet his gaze. But he didn't blame her for her brother-in-law's behavior.

"Kade said he called one right after Lexie found us together. I'm furious, Julian. I mean, Lexie *knew.* My own sister knew and didn't tell me."

She rose to her feet, coming up beside him and placing a hand on his shoulder. He welcomed the contact, as innocuous as it happened to be.

"I'm sorry," she said. "I had no idea they'd go to such ridiculous, insulting lengths. They had no right to invade your privacy that way."

She was correct about that. Anger and disbelief swirled inside him, along with a bone-deep weariness that he had a hunch wouldn't go away for a long time. Nothing he did, said, or had become made a difference to his one-time friend.

Before he could think things through more, Kendall continued. "I'm so hurt. I told them to trust my judgment. That you've proven yourself to me, and by extension, that should be good enough for them."

"But it wasn't."

"No," she agreed.

And it never would be, he thought. Because if Kade was willing to go so far as to have him spied on, hoping to find something to use against him, he'd never accept him in Kendall's life. The knife in his back might be deserved after what he'd done to Kade, but at this point, when was penance enough?

Kendall looked at him with sad eyes. "And the irony is they think they have something on you. Something that should convince me you're toxic and I need to steer clear."

He let out a harsh, disbelieving laugh since he'd been nothing but a choir boy in the short time since Lexie walked through Kendall's door and Kade had him watched.

"And what did he find?" Julian asked.

"He said a drug addict and ex-con has been coming by your apartment all weekend. And the fact that you're hanging around and exposed to that kind of person when you have an addiction makes you bad for me."

"And destined to use again, is that it?" Fury spun through his veins. "He has no idea how hard I worked to get clean. How determined I am to stay that way."

"It's Billy, isn't it, who's been coming around?" Kendall asked.

"Yeah."

"I thought he was pretty clear that he didn't want to be a brother to Alex?"

He blew out a long breath. "I'm sure Kade would be thrilled to know Billy came by to ask his eighteen-year-old sister to get people at school to come to him for drugs. Isn't that fucking great?"

"Are you kidding me? That poor kid!" Kendall shook her head and wrapped her arms around herself tight.

"She was beside herself. I managed to calm Alex down and get ahold of Billy's parole officer. I hope the bastard gets himself arrested. He hasn't been around since she turned him down. It just took him awhile to catch her at home, so he kept coming over, and that's what Kade's investigator saw."

She inclined her head in understanding. "I knew

there was an explanation," she murmured.

He blinked in surprise. "You believed in me?"

"Of course I did!"

Sweet relief coursed through him even as he comprehended the truth. "But that doesn't matter." Not to Kade. Not to her sister, the people who mattered most in her life.

She narrowed her gaze. "Why not? I'm telling you that I believe in you. I'm here, aren't I? If this is because I took some time away from you, I'm sorry but—"

"It's not about that."

He stepped forward, took her hand, knowing that what he was about to do next would hurt her as much as it would devastate him. He just didn't see any way around it.

"Then what is it about? Why doesn't me believing in you matter?"

"It matters to me, more than you can possibly know." Nobody had had faith in him for most of his life, except his sister.

Kendall's belief meant everything. *She* meant everything to him, and because of that, he'd take care of her the only way he knew how. Even if it meant destroying a part of himself in the process.

"It's about your sister and Kade—and your relationship with them." He ran his thumbs over the tops of her hands, the touch so important to him. It would probably be his last. "You explained it to me. How much you need them in your life, and believe me when I tell you, I get it. I'd feel the same way if the situation were reversed and it was my sister. But I also now get there is no pleasing them or earning back trust."

She opened and closed her mouth before speaking. "You don't know that for sure. Given time—"

He shook his head. "I know it. Kade proved it. A PI?"

For Julian it was the last straw.

He'd apologized and he was a different person, but he still had his pride, and Julian sure as fuck wouldn't grovel to Kade. Not that it would matter if he did. Kade would make it his mission to break up him and Kendall and destroy all the good things between them. He'd rather she have some positive memories of him than all shitty ones after Kade got through pitting them against each other and destroying what they shared.

He glanced down at their entwined hands. "I know what your sister, your twin, means to you. I won't come between you, and I won't make you choose."

No decent human being would do that to her. Julian might not be perfect, but he wouldn't hurt her that way. Better for him to break it off now and let her return to the life, the family she needed.

She blinked, her eyes watery, as comprehension dawned. "Just so I'm not making assumptions, you need to spell out exactly what you are saying."

"I love you, Kendall, but this can't work. Us." He stepped back, putting distance between them because if he didn't, he'd pull her into his arms and never let her go. "*We* can't work," he said, tearing out his own heart in the process.

Her eyes opened wide. "You tell me you love me while you're breaking up with me?" Her voice rose, almost shattering his resolve to do what was best for her.

"I have to." If an apology wasn't good enough for Kade, if Kendall's word wasn't enough of a damned referral, if he was going to continue to look for things to nail Julian with, then he was out of options.

The kindest thing he could do for Kendall was to let her go, because if they stayed together, the family rift would only breed resentment. "I'm not going to force you to choose me or your family. I know what that will do to you. It isn't fair of me to ask."

Tears were in her eyes, then dripping down her face. "So instead you'll take the choice out of my hands? God!" She stomped toward the door. "What did I do in my life that everyone thinks they can make my choices for me?"

He'd followed her to the entryway. "Kendall—"

"No. Lexie, I understand a little why she's still making my choices for me. She's had to clean up my messes for years, but you? I thought you respected me more than that."

"I do. That's why I have to do this." But a little voice in his head asked if that was really true. If maybe he was sending her away not as much for her own good as for his.

Because *he* was the one afraid of being hurt when she walked away, weeks or even months down the road, when the family pressure became too much for her to bear.

She looked at him, hurt and betrayal in her gaze. "You keep telling yourself you did it for me, but it's a lie and a cop-out. You're afraid to face them by my side," she said, her parting shot hitting hard before she grabbed the knob and stormed out, taking his heart with her.

No sooner had Kendall walked out of Julian's apartment than he headed for the family room, picked up a glass of water he'd had earlier, and threw it against the wall in frustration and pain.

Before Lexie walked in on them at Kendall's apartment, he'd been living in a bubble, ignoring the outside world, and happy to do it for too damned long.

Had he really thought he could have everything he

wanted? When had life ever worked that way for him?

This thing he was building with Kendall, it was *real*.

And now it was over.

And he only had himself to blame. Kendall had a valid point. One that had begun to creep in the closer she walked to the door.

He was the coward.

He was the one afraid, while she'd been willing to fight for them. By his side.

Julian hadn't wanted the high of drugs since he'd quit. He hadn't needed the escape they offered.

Until now.

He hated feeling powerless, and that's exactly the situation he was in. He'd given up everything he wanted for his future, let go of the woman he loved, and why? To make life easier? Or because he was afraid? Afraid to believe the world could hold good things for him? Afraid to believe he deserved them.

He ran a shaking hand through his hair. He hadn't thought of himself during all this because blaming her family, giving her what she needed seemed easier than facing his own failings. And Lord knew he had many.

After promising he'd never hurt her again, that was exactly what he'd done. In the name of what was best for her.

But did the reasons really matter? The end result was inevitable at some point in the future anyway.

Thanks to Lexie. And Kade. In time Kendall would realize he'd done her a favor. She'd have her family, her twin, her life. And he'd be alone.

Fuck.

He wished he had another glass within reach that he could throw against the damned wall. He didn't. So instead of more destruction, instead of finding someone like Billy for a fix, he grabbed his keys and headed to a meeting.

Because the only way he had a chance of keeping what was left of his life together was to stay on his current path and stay clean.

Even if he was alone.

★ ★ ★

KENDALL HEADED DIRECTLY home from Julian's, operating on autopilot, not letting herself think or feel, because if she did, she'd break down in the cab on the way to her apartment. She somehow managed to wait until she was safely inside before she let the pain go.

She leaned back against the door and slid to the floor, crying big, gulping, heaving sobs. She braced her arms on her knees, resting her head and allowing all the feelings she'd held back to surface.

Waffles, who'd come bounding over to greet her, licked her face and her tears with her rough tongue. Kendall was so heartbroken she couldn't even bring herself to laugh at her dog's antics. Instead she pulled Waffles close, taking comfort in her soft fur and warm body.

How had things fallen apart so badly? Probably a stupid question. A part of her had known all along it would end this way, but she'd been in denial, wanting to think her twin would choose Kendall's happiness over the bitterness and anger of Kade and Julian's ugly past. Especially when both Lexie and Kade saw how much Julian had changed. But they wouldn't even consider the possibility.

And then Julian had taken himself out of the relationship without even giving them a chance to face the world together. Come what may.

As she'd stood in that office and listened to Kade and Lexie basically undermine her judgment, her self-esteem, the very core of who she was today, she'd known. If push came to shove, if she had to choose, she'd pick Julian. She'd even warned her twin not to put her in that position.

Because Kendall deserved a happy, fulfilling life as much as her sister did. And when she'd almost lost Kade thanks to Kendall, what had Lexie done? She'd decided it was time to live her own life.

Kendall had wanted to do the same. And she'd intended to tell Julian just that. She'd even started to try—until he'd done the same thing her twin had. He'd taken her choices away from her.

Despite the fact that he, of all people, understood what it was like to fight to come back from rock bottom, to be a new and different person, capable of making good, strong decisions, he'd ended things.

Because he was afraid. She'd seen it in his eyes, his expression when he'd let her go. It had been easier to break things off now than to go through the fire together. Maybe he didn't trust they were strong enough to come out the other side. Or maybe he just didn't believe in himself.

She was so disappointed in him.

So hurt.

So destroyed.

Because he loved her... and she loved him, too, very much, and yet he hadn't given her a chance to even say the words before he'd ripped everything she wanted in life away from her.

She wiped her tears on her bare arms and rose to her feet, heading to the bathroom for a tissue. Somehow, she made it through the rest of the day. It helped that she did a grocery run and returned with pints of mint chocolate chip ice cream to binge on in her despair.

Her cell rang, and a quick glance told her it was Lexie calling. Kendall had nothing to say to her sister, so she sent the call directly to message. She needed to calm down before she could have a rational conversation with her twin.

When the texts began coming in, too, Kendall shut off her cell. She knew Julian meant what he said and *he* wouldn't be texting or calling to say he'd changed his mind. So she didn't want to talk to anyone right now.

She cried herself to sleep, and by the next morning, a healthy anger at Lexie and Kade and Julian had taken over the pain and crying. She was furious at their audacity to make decisions for her. To run her life. To not believe in her enough.

But she still had a job to do, so she headed to work and spent the morning in the back rooms of the shelter cleaning out the stalls with a garden hose. There were a lot of unglamorous parts of the job, and she did them all. She didn't object to the mindless chore. Someone had to clean and it gave her time to think.

Except today there was nothing she wanted to dwell on. Josie sensed her mood, asked her if she wanted to talk, and when Kendall declined, she left her to her own thoughts.

After she finished in the stalls, she returned to the front office to complete more of the paperwork from the dog transfers this past weekend.

When her cell rang, her instinct was to automatically send it to voice mail, but instead she glanced down, surprised to see Alex's name on the screen.

"Hello?" Kendall asked, resting an elbow on the desk as she spoke.

"Hi, Kendall?"

"Hi, Alex. How are you?" she asked.

"Umm, good. Listen, you said I could come to you for anything, right?" Her voice sounded uncertain.

"Of course. What's up?"

Alex cleared her throat. "A guy asked me out, I said yes, and now I have nothing to wear on the date," she said in a rush, as if she was embarrassed and had to spit out all the information at once, before she lost her nerve. "I never really had someone to help me with girl stuff. Would you come shopping with me?"

Relieved it was something so easy, Kendall answered immediately. "Of course I'll go with you." Considering it could have been a call about Alex's brother, Kendall considered this request a win.

She'd be happy to help Alex find something for a date. Not only would it boost the young girl's self-esteem to have something new and pretty, the shopping trip would be a great distraction for Kendall. One she needed badly.

"Thank you," Alex said on a huge, relieved exhale. "I mean, I couldn't ask Julian to go with me, that would be so weird, and I had no idea what to buy if I went alone."

Kendall laughed, ignoring the pang in her chest at just the mention of Julian's name. She wondered if Alex knew they'd broken up. Regardless, she was glad the young girl felt comfortable enough to turn to her when she needed something.

"When can you go?" Kendall asked.

They made plans for tomorrow night after they both got off work, and Kendall disconnected the call.

Her life might have gone to hell, but at least Alex's was looking up.

★　★　★

A WEEK HAD gone by since Julian let Kendall walk out of his life. Technically he'd sent her away. And he was still wrestling with why he'd done it. Who he was protecting? Her? Or himself?

He didn't like the answer he came up with, but he was no closer to knowing how to fix the mess he'd made of his life.

He wasn't in the mood for a meal now, but Nick insisted they meet at the place they usually chose after a meeting.

The man always knew when Julian was floundering. Everyone should have such a solid friend.

"So you fucked things up with Kendall?" Nick asked bluntly before he even sat down. He settled into the booth and eyed Julian with concern.

"What makes you think that?"

Nick set both arms on the table and leaned forward. "I haven't heard from you in a week, and you canceled dinner Sunday night by calling Lauren and leaving a message on her cell. None of which is like you. So something's wrong, and the only thing I can come up with is Kendall. She's the one with the power to hurt you."

"And yet you think I'm the one who fucked it up?"

"Did you?" Nick asked.

"Yes. In a big way." Julian ran a hand through his hair. "I haven't slept. I've barely eaten. I just—"

Nick picked up a butter knife and twirled it in his hands. "Slow it down and tell me. I'll understand. Because if you think my road to happiness with my wife was easy, you're wrong. I was an alcoholic from the time I was in my teens. She had a lot to put up with before and after I sobered up. So I understand mistakes better than most."

"Can I take your order?" the waitress who had walked over to the table asked.

"Please give us a minute," Julian said. He waited until she stepped away and glanced at Nick. "I broke it off because Kade will never come around. He hired a PI to check up on me and will do anything to keep me away from her. If I stayed, it would be like forcing her to choose between me and her twin. Nobody should have to do that, especially not Kendall." Not when friends were hard to come by and she had her own struggles in life.

"Hmm. And what did she say about this… magnanimous, asinine gesture?" Nick asked, calling it as he saw it.

As it was.

Julian winced. "She all but called me a coward."

Nick burst out laughing. "I knew I liked that girl." He sobered, his smile leaving his face. "Now tell me why you really sent her away."

Julian roughly exhaled. "Didn't you ever hear of preemptive behavior? It was going to come to this eventually. I just did it before she resented me, not after." The words sounded thick and untrue on his tongue.

Nick shook his head. "Really?" He obviously didn't buy it, either.

"No. I mean I don't want her to have to choose. It hurts me to think of doing that to her, but that's not the main reason I ended things. I did it because it's going to hurt a fuck of a lot more when she ultimately walks away the longer we stay together."

"Aha. So you are a coward." Nick pointed at him accusingly with the butter knife.

"Fuck you."

"For being right?"

And that was why Nick was such a reliable friend. Julian could count on him to hit him where it hurt and make him face a truth that had been circling in his head all week.

Julian groaned. "To make matters worse, I haven't called her in a week. I thought I was doing us both a favor but damn. I fucked up. I miss her. And I don't want Kade dictating how I live my life. Nobody should have that kind of power over another human being. I screwed up, but I don't deserve that kind of punishment forever."

"No, they shouldn't," Nick agreed. "But as for Kade, I'm not sure he's the villain you're making him out to be. Put yourself in his place. Your sister-in-law comes to you and says trust me, this guy who screwed you over is really a good man. You're going to just buy into it?"

"No." Julian pinched the bridge of his nose. He had to make this better.

He needed Kendall in his life, and she needed him in hers.

"You have a plan?" Nick asked.

Julian rolled his head, the muscles in his neck and shoulders stiff. Although he'd waited a week, though he'd wallowed in self-pity, in the back of his mind, he'd known all along what he needed to do.

He'd just needed time to put the pieces together in

his mind, to work out his own demons in his head. "I plan to let Kade know I'm not going to back down—and that I mean it this time. That I'm in it for the long haul. That's the only way to prove I'm the man I say I am."

"And then?" Nick asked, an approving grin on his face.

"I'll go get my girl."

Chapter Fourteen

S HOPPING WITH AN eighteen-year-old girl was not for the weak. Together Kendall and Alex hit many small boutique stores in Soho that were reasonably priced and some better-known chain stores. Alex tried on more clothes than Kendall owned—and shopping sprees had been her Achilles' heel during her improperly or unmedicated days. Her father had paid off many a ridiculous bill, she thought, flushing with pained embarrassment at the memory.

Finally Alex chose a floral summer dress with a halter top and a pair of sandals with a chunky high heel. She was riding the high of success Kendall remembered well but no longer felt. She was just happy and living vicariously through Alex's excitement for her date.

When they parted ways, they were still downtown. Alex headed uptown to the library to work, and Kendall decided, since she was in the neighborhood, to pay her sister and her brother-in-law a visit.

She'd managed to cut Lexie short whenever she called this past week, needing time to nurse her anger and hurt and to think about what she wanted to say and how she wanted to handle the situation before she just blurted out mean-spirited things she couldn't take back and really didn't mean. Her therapy appointments had also helped put things into perspective.

She was still hurt by Julian. Incredibly hurt, but her anger had dissipated in light of serious thought and understanding. He had his issues like she did. And she knew he was afraid she'd choose her sister over him.

After all, she'd pulled away and spelled out her deep need not to disappoint her twin. He was just giving her what she thought she needed... also reacting to his own fears and a healthy dose of uncertainty and distrust of people in general, Kade especially.

Did she blame him for breaking up with her if he really loved her like he claimed? Yes, yes she did. But a part of her understood the need to do it before what he thought was inevitable happened—she left him—and it hurt even more.

She'd given him a week and was debating going over to see him and make him confront what was between them. If he really did love her, how could he walk away?

But first she had something to settle with her sister and brother-in-law.

When she arrived at Blink, Lexie was in Kade's office with the door open, so Kendall knocked.

"Come on in," Kade called.

"Kendall!" Lexie was on her feet and hugging her before Kendall could draw a breath, her arms holding on tight.

Kendall swallowed an onslaught of emotion and wrapped her arms around her sister, too.

"I'm sorry," Lexie said. "We went too far and I'm sorry." Her voice wobbled with the same emotion running through Kendall.

"I wouldn't say too far but... I'm sorry I upset you," Kade said, sounding like the words were pulled from him but no less heartfelt. She didn't expect him to regret his intrusive behavior. It was his way of looking out for her even if she didn't like it.

"Thank you," she murmured.

Kendall stepped away from her twin and brushed at her damp eyes. "I came to tell you guys a few things, and I need you to hear me."

"I'm listening," Lexie assured her. She stepped over to Kade, lacing her hand through his and clearly giving him a squeeze.

"Of course I'm listening. And I'm hearing you," he promised.

Kendall smiled in thanks and turned to her sister. "Okay, well, first, you should know I will always be eternally grateful for all you did for me, all you sacrificed, and all you gave up to try and keep me on a sane, healthy path. I will never forget it, and I want to think I'd do the same for you."

Lexie nodded, the emotion clear in her expression. "I love you."

Kendall swallowed hard. "Me, too. That's why this next part is so hard for me to say, but here goes. I'm an adult now. And yes, I've made mistakes, and yes, I've been ill, but I'm better and I've proven that by now. I take my medicine every day. I'm in therapy. If I feel off and it goes on too long, I let my doctor know and ask for a medication adjustment. I'm living as good a life as I can."

Lexie sniffed. "I know. I see it and I'm so incredibly proud of you."

Kendall straightened her shoulders. "Then don't make me pay for my bipolar disorder and my past. Maybe you couldn't trust my judgment then, but you can now."

"Kendall, it isn't you we don't trust," Kade said.

She rubbed her hands together in front of her. "Well, then that brings me to my next point. You got your way. Julian walked away from me in part because he doesn't want to make me choose between him and my family." Intense pain racked her as she said those words out loud.

Kade opened his mouth to speak, and Lexie elbowed him hard in the side. "Shut up. Don't say a word to her about how it's for the best. She doesn't think so, and that's what matters." Lexie met her twin's gaze.

Kendall knew that was Lexie's way of saying she'd do her best to respect Kendall's independence and needs, and she was grateful.

"I was just going to say I'm sorry," Kade muttered.

"Sorry and I'm sure relieved," Kendall said. Because Kade had to be happy Julian had broken up with her. But she wasn't finished.

"And now my final point. I don't want things to be over with Julian, and if I have my way, they won't be because I love him. Which means you can accept my decision and be part of my life, or you can lose me. The choice is yours. I'm finished letting anyone, no matter how well meaning, decide the direction of my life. Not even my twin. Or her husband." She finished in a rush and folded her arms across her chest, glancing from Lexie, whose eyes were open wide, to Kade, who appeared surprised.

Kendall's pulse pounded and nerves made her dizzy, but she'd made her stand. She'd be lying if she didn't say she was panicked at the thought of losing her twin for good, of being stripped of her support system and left alone. But she had to be strong.

The ball was in their court.

"Well?" A way-too-familiar voice asked from behind her. "She wants you to respect her wishes and let her be with the man she loves."

Kendall gasped, both at Julian's unexpected arrival and his use of *that* word as applied to her. She'd never told him she loved him.

She spun around to find him in the doorway, one shoulder propped on the frame, a pleased, happy smile on his handsome face. And oh, did he look good in his black tee shirt and sexy bulging muscles, his dark jeans molded to his strong thighs. She'd missed him so much.

"How long have you been standing there?" she asked.

"Long enough to know you love me and want me back. And long enough to realize you're stronger and braver than I was. But that's about to change because I came here to tell Kade the same thing." He straightened his shoulders and stepped into the room, clearly prepared to stand up to Kade.

"I thought we had that conversation," Kade said, reminding him. "And what did you do? You promised you were a good guy, and then you walked away from her." Kade folded his arms across his chest and raised an accusing eyebrow his way.

Julian didn't flinch, accepting his behavior and Kade's words. "That was an impulsive, stupid response to your private investigator. I'll tell you what. If you want to know something about my life, ask me. I'm an open book these days. Don't go behind my back for information and don't tell the woman I love that I'm no good for her. Because you're damn well wrong."

Warmth and gratitude rushed through Kendall as Julian stood up for her to her family. It was everything she'd ever wanted to see and hear.

"Looks like you two made your choices," Kade said.

Kendall couldn't breathe at the implication in those words. Was he really going to cut her out of his life? And what about Lexie?

"Kade!" her twin said, obviously just as shocked.

"What? I'm about to offer them my office to work out whatever is going on between them."

Kendall's heart began to beat again, although erratically. "You're not... You aren't turning your back on me?" she asked.

"Oh, honey," Lexie said. "That was never our intention. We want what's best for you. We just couldn't understand that you chose... him. But now that you have, we'll have to find a way to make it work. I can't lose you, either."

"Oh my God." Kendall knew Julian was standing there, that he loved her, that he'd come to fight for her. But she hugged her twin first anyway because for a split second… well, she didn't want to think about that ever again.

"Come on, let's leave them alone," Lexie said, walking to Kade, grasping his hand, and leading him out.

Kade came to a halt in front of Julian. Two self-assured, commanding men. "Hurt her and you answer to me."

A few seconds of silence passed, in which Kendall once again held her breath.

"I accept those terms," Julian finally said, extending a hand for Kade to shake.

Kade glanced down… and completed the gesture, causing grateful tears to fill Kendall's eyes. She glanced at her sister, who was equally touched and affected.

She knew better than to think everything was perfect, but they'd forged a truce, and that was all she could hope for right now. Time would prove to her sister and Kade that Julian was honorable and trustworthy.

As Kade and Lexie walked out of his office, Kade turned back. "Don't *do* anything in here. I don't think my anxiety or OCD could handle the thought." And then he was gone and they were alone.

★ ★ ★

JULIAN WAITED FOR Kade and Lexie to walk out the

door before locking it behind them. He wasn't so much shutting them out as closing Kendall in. To say this afternoon hadn't gone the way he'd expected was an understatement.

He'd been prepared for a fight or, at the very least, an argument.

What he hadn't been prepared to see or hear was Kendall standing up to her sister and Kade—who was intimidating on his best day—for him. Kendall, declaring her love for him, consequences be damned. His girl was brave. Braver than he was, and he was humbled by it all. And he couldn't wait another minute to touch her again.

He turned, and before he knew it, she'd bolted forward and jumped into his arms.

He caught her, stumbling back before he could steady himself, and looked into her eyes. "Jesus, I was a fucking moron."

She laced her fingers behind his neck to hold on. "I think I gave you plenty of reason to think breaking up with me was the right thing to do." She bit down on her lower lip, something he would much rather be the one doing. "But don't try something like that again. From now on we communicate. Agreed?"

He answered by sealing his lips over hers and kissing her for all he was worth, breathing her in as if he couldn't get enough. Because he couldn't. He'd missed her touch, her scent, the very essence of her being, and he never wanted to let her go.

He slid his fingers through her hair and slicked his tongue past her parted lips. She moaned and kissed him back, all the while holding him close.

His cock throbbed inside his jeans, reminding him of Kade's warning, and unbidden, a laugh bubbled up in his throat.

"Oh my God. What's so funny?" she asked, her eyes twinkling with relief and happiness. A happiness that matched his.

"I was just thinking about what Kade said about us not doing anything in his office."

A smile tweaked her lips. "You so want to do it on his desk, don't you?"

"Don't give me any ideas, you bad girl. The man's just given me a partial opening. I don't want to screw it up." He grew more serious, gazing into her eyes. "You're too important to me. I love you, Kendall."

She brushed her thumb over his cheek. "I love you, too. Enough to risk everything."

"I won't let you regret it. I'm all in. I promise. No walking away, backing out, or doing something stupid to screw things up. I'm in too deep."

She grinned. "I'm glad to hear it because I'm in deep, too. And I'm not going anywhere, either."

Epilogue

MIRACLES DID HAPPEN and today was proof.

Thanksgiving, a year and three months after Kendall and Julian first reunited, Kendall invited everyone over to their new house for the holiday. As she set the table and got everything ready, she trembled, knowing she had so much to be grateful for.

She looked around *her kitchen*, in *her house*, in a neighborhood with a cul-de-sac on the same street as Nick and Lauren, in renewed disbelief. A glance at the wedding ring on her finger was yet another shock every time she looked down… and she'd been blissfully, happily married for four months.

Was it fast? Yes. Was it right? Without a doubt.

The fact that Kade and Lexie and their six-month-old baby, Matthew, and the other Blink partners had agreed to join them for the holiday was nothing short of a miracle. One she would never take for granted. And neither would Julian, who was outside placing the turkey in the deep fryer.

He was a different man now. A happy man who'd stopped kicking himself for his past mistakes and who rarely looked back, unless it was to acknowledge how much better his life was today.

Along with the Blink contingent, Julian's sister was coming, as were Lauren, Nick, and Brian. Alex was upstairs and her boyfriend would join them, too.

She was a flexible kid, she'd had to be after all her moving around in foster care, and so she'd been willing to switch schools for her senior year. She was brave. And it had worked out. She'd made a few select friends and even met a boy. She'd applied to colleges and was going to New York University next year, smart girl, living in a dorm, and her entire life would change.

Thanks to Julian.

And in January, Kendall was starting classes to become a vet tech. She was following her dreams, with Julian's encouragement.

"How's my beautiful wife?" Julian asked, walking into the kitchen.

She'd never get used to seeing him, his handsome face smiling at her, the sexy scruff, the enticing muscles in his forearms, even in a long-sleeve waffle-textured shirt.

"Hi." She smiled and walked into his arms. "Everyone will be here in an hour."

"Is Alyssa bringing Blackie?" he asked of his sister's emotional-support dog.

As Kendall had hoped, one of the dogs from the Maryland trip, a black Labrador mix, had the temperament to be matched for Alyssa's needs. She'd named him accordingly, because it was an easy name to remember. All she had to do was look at her dog.

"She is. Waffles and Steve will have company. Where are they, anyway?"

"Out back." In the fenced yard.

Really, could life get any sweeter? There had been a time when she'd been spiraling, and any kind of calm and happiness had seemed out of reach. But with the patience and support of her twin and the right treatment, she'd found a peace she'd never imagined possible.

She leaned back and tipped her head back so Julian could kiss her lips. "I love you, Julian Dane."

"I love you back, Kendall Dane."

★ ★ ★

Five Years Later

THEY NEEDED A bigger house, Julian decided, as he slowly dipped the turkey into the fryer. Tradition was a wonderful thing, and Thanksgiving at his and Kendall's house had become the custom for her family and his.

He glanced over to where his ten-year-old foster son, Jonah, was playing fetch with Steve and Waffles, successfully with Steve, not so much with the fur ball who preferred to roll around with the stick or ball. Kendall was inside with Randi, their thirteen-year-old foster daughter, setting the table for their guests.

He and Kendall had made a conscious decision to foster children who didn't have a home. After talking to various doctors, they decided that going off her medication presented too big a risk of re-hospitalization. Statistics weren't always right, but Kendall felt strongly about not taking that chance, and he respected whatever she wanted to do. They both knew they had enough love to give, and they could make up their family the way they wanted to.

Never in his wildest dreams had he imagined he'd have a family of his own. Not growing up with his alcoholic mother, nor during his drug days, which were long past, although he still attended a monthly meeting.

And he certainly never thought he'd have a friendship with Kade, Derek, and Lucas, but he did. It was no longer a hesitant, wary tolerance.

Bygones really were bygones.

Kendall joined him outside, wrapping her arms around his waist.

"Eew!" Jonah said, coming up behind him.

He rolled his eyes. He loved his wife, so sue him. He wrapped an arm around Kendall's waist. "What do you say to house hunting? We're outgrowing this place," he said as Steve ran by, Waffles merely staring from across the lawn.

"Works for me. I just don't want to move far from work."

She had a job as a vet tech at a local veterinarian's that gave her flexible morning hours and enabled her to be home after school. And since Julian still worked out of the house, someone was around in the mornings to get the kids out the door.

It all worked.

Because they trusted each other.

Loved each other.

And were still as deeply in love with each other as they'd been the day they admitted it out loud.

Stay tuned for Carly's next super sexy read, **TAKE ME AGAIN** and read on for more information including an excerpt!

TAKE ME AGAIN

He's used to getting what he wants... but she's going to make him work for it.

Sebastian Knight is a closer. Be it a real estate deal or the woman of his choice, everything he wants is his for the taking.

Sexy and irresistible, a wink, a smile, or a handshake always seals the deal.

Until everything unravels around him.

After Ashley Easton's social climbing mother married into the Knight family, Ashley knew better than to get involved with sexy, trouble making Sebastian Knight but their attraction is undeniable, their chemistry intense, and in a moment of weakness, she turns to him, a mistake that cost her her home and her family. After she was sent away, she swore she'd never come back.

Sebastian never expected to see Ashley, the one woman he's never been able to get over, again.

When she walks back into his life at the worst possible time, more beautiful than ever, he's ready for a second chance. She's sassy and sexy everything he's ever desired. And she's back for good. Except Ashley wants nothing to do with the playboy who broke her heart. Too bad his sex appeal makes it harder and harder to keep him at arm's length.

Sebastian Knight might have a talent for sealing the deal but this is one game he's going to have to work to win.

TAKE ME AGAIN

Chapter One

SEBASTIAN KNIGHT'S HEAD pounded like a motherfucker, and light streamed in from the window, piercing through one eye and into his brain.

He groaned and rolled over, burying his face in the pillow. At twenty-six, wasn't he too damned old for a hangover like this? Yeah, he'd have to remember that the next time he picked up a glass of tequila and asked the bartender to keep them coming to celebrate closing a huge deal with his brothers for their tech company, Knight Time Technology. Except Ethan and Parker had gone home after toasting their success. After that, Sebastian didn't remember much.

A flash of red flickered through his mind. A woman with flame-hued hair had joined him at the bar. He recalled the unusual color and the obviously fake but very tempting breasts that protruded over the top of her tight dress, along with his body's reaction to her assets.

Shit.

Was he alone now?

He lifted his head and opened his eyes, not seeing anyone lying beside him and not recognizing where he was, but from the abundance of white furniture and the generic feel and look of the place, it was definitely a hotel room. An upscale suite but a hotel nevertheless.

Memory came back in small increments.

The deal they'd landed was to supply state-of-the-art locks to a defense contractor. They'd outbid some major players when Sebastian had stepped in and closed the deal, something he excelled at and his brothers counted on him to do.

They'd headed to The Bar at the Baccarat Hotel in order to celebrate. Toasted their success. He'd taken his first sip of Don Julio 1942, and it had gone down smooth.

And though he might not remember making the elevator ride up to this hotel room, he was here. Which meant *he'd* be the one making his escape from this one-night stand, hopefully without too much of a scene.

The click of a door sounded, and the redhead walked out of the bathroom, a towel wrapped around her body. Her cleavage was as ample as he remembered, her hair as red, her face? Not as pretty as he'd have hoped or as she'd probably appeared to his drunk self.

He scrubbed a hand over his gritty eyes and pushed up to a sitting position.

"Morning, lover." She started toward him, her stride confident, but he wasn't in the mood for small talk or sex.

Instead of waiting for her to ease onto the mattress alongside him, he slid out of bed and rose to his feet. He glanced down to find his pants, grateful to see a torn condom package on the floor beside his clothes. Thank God, even in his inebriated state, he'd been smart about wrapping up.

"Aren't you going to stick around for a morning quickie?" she asked as she opened the towel, revealing her naked body, his for the taking.

His dick didn't even perk up at the sight of her tits, and he shook his head. "Sorry, doll," he said, because he didn't remember her name, dressing as he spoke. "I have a meeting I need to get to."

Her pout was real. "Didn't you have a good time last night?" she asked, sounding hurt, fumbling to cover herself with the towel again in the face of his rejection.

I don't remember wasn't what she wanted to hear.

He zipped his trousers and slid on his white dress shirt, buttoning up. "It was great. But now it's over," he said, knowing he had to be very clear about his intentions or lack thereof. Socks and shoes went on next, and he was dressed and ready to go.

He patted his pockets, double-checking for his wallet and cell phone, and headed for the door. As awkward as this was, no need to prolong it or make it worse.

"Bastard," she muttered.

And after he'd pulled the door closed, he heard what sounded like a shoe being thrown as the door clicked shut behind him. Yeah, he really was getting too old for this shit.

He pulled out his phone, only to discover he'd turned off the ringer sometime during the night and his brothers had tried to reach him numerous times. So had his younger sister, Sierra.

He narrowed his gaze. Why the hell had everyone been looking for him?

He took the elevator down to the first floor and walked through the lobby, across the white marble, and out into the Manhattan sunshine before hitting redial and calling his oldest brother, Ethan. When the call went directly to voicemail, he dialed Parker next.

"Where the fuck have you been?" his middle sibling all but yelled.

"Calm yourself, Switzerland," he said, using the nickname the family had for Parker that had begun during his championship skiing days and stuck because he refused to take sides in family arguments, always tending to remain neutral. "I'm here now. What's going on?"

Squinting into the sun, Sebastian hailed the first empty cab he saw, the driver coming to a skidding stop on his side of the street.

"Mandy died, Sebastian."

He froze, his hand on the taxi door handle. "Say that again."

"Mandy died," he said of Ethan's wife. "I've been with E all night. So has Sierra. So get your ass to his place, like, yesterday."

The cab driver honked the horn, letting Sebastian know he'd better climb in the back seat or the man would take off. He opened the door and slid onto the taped-up pleather, his heart heavy and thudding inside his chest.

"What happened?" he asked through his thick throat and dry mouth.

Everyone loved Ethan's wife, Amanda, Mandy for short, who had been an executive at Knight Time Technology.

"Buddy, where to?" the cab driver asked impatiently.

He gave the address of the apartment building uptown that the company owned, where all the siblings resided.

Parker waited for Sebastian to finish before he answered. "Accidental overdose."

"What the fuck?" Mandy didn't take drugs, not that he knew of.

"It's a long story." Parker sounded exhausted. "Just come home and I'll explain everything."

"How's Ethan?" he asked, worried about his older brother, who felt it was his job to look after everyone else.

He'd taken on the role of caretaker after their mother passed away when Sebastian had been fifteen.

Only nineteen at the time, Ethan had stepped up because, frankly, their father had never been the responsible parent.

"About as good as you'd expect," Parker muttered.

Which meant not good at all.

He needed to get to his sibling, but the Manhattan traffic moved at a snail's pace and the ride seemed to take forever. He closed his eyes throughout the trip uptown and pictured Ethan's wife, a petite brunette with a vibrant personality. Granted, she'd been more subdued lately, her shoulder surgery almost two years ago having been hard on her physically and mentally. But an accidental overdose? It didn't compute.

The cab finally came to a stop. He shoved his credit card into the slot and completed the transaction, climbed out of the car, and made his way past the doorman, into the building and up the elevator, another ride that seemed endless.

Arriving at Ethan's door, he knocked once and Sierra let him in, wrapping her arms around him, her smaller body shaking as she cried. The Knight siblings were each two years apart and he was close to his twenty-four-year-old baby sister. He walked into the apartment, Sierra holding on to him, and found his brothers in the living room.

She stepped away, sniffing as she sank into an oversized chair. From his place on the sofa, Ethan rose to his feet. His brother's dark hair was disheveled, his eyes bloodshot and red.

In silence, Sebastian stepped forward and pulled him into a brotherly embrace. "I'm sorry, man," he said at last. "What happened?"

Ethan straightened to his full height. "I came home. Thought she was napping but I couldn't wake her up. I called 911 but it was too late." His voice sounded like gravel, the pain etched in his face raw and real.

"Parker–" Sebastian gestured to his brother, who was now sitting on the far side of the couch. "Parker said it was an overdose, but I don't understand. Overdose on what?"

"Sit," Ethan said and Sebastian chose a matching chair next to Sierra's. "It was Oxy."

"What?" He couldn't believe what he was hearing.

Ethan shook his head, obviously at a loss.

"It started after the shoulder surgery," Parker said, taking over when Ethan's voice failed him. "The doctors loaded her up with drugs to help with the pain. We had no idea they kept giving them to her until she was hooked."

Sebastian blinked in surprise, whether at Mandy's addiction he'd known nothing about or his middle brother's use of the word *we* when describing the situation, he couldn't be sure. The one thing Sebastian did know, he wasn't part of that *we*.

"Shit. I'm sorry." He ran a hand through his already disheveled hair.

As he began to put the pieces together of the story his brother was telling him, Sebastian reeled with what, so far, had gone unsaid. "You aren't shocked by this, and not because Ethan told you last night, after Mandy died." From the matter-of-fact way Parker had relayed the information, as if he'd already digested it and it had settled inside him, it was obvious. "You've known all along."

Parker merely nodded.

He glanced at his sister, who sat wide-eyed on the chair next to his. "What about you? Did you know?" he asked.

She swallowed hard. "Mandy told me recently that she was having problems. I talked to Ethan about it," she admitted.

"So everyone knew something. But me." Sebastian rose to his feet, hurt and betrayal warring with anger, combining with grief inside him.

Parker met his gaze. "I was there the first time he found her pills. That's all."

But Sebastian sensed there was more to it. That he'd been left out of the loop for a reason. He glanced at Ethan.

"We didn't want to bother you with serious shit,"

Ethan said. "You didn't *need* to know. We were handling it."

"I didn't need to know or you didn't trust me to keep it to myself?" Sebastian asked, the truth crystallizing without his brother having to say anything. "Admit it. You were afraid I'd share info, like the Williamson deal."

It'd been his first year in the family business, one started by their great-great-grandfather, who'd been a locksmith. Legend had it he'd been such an expert on locks, he'd broken Billy the Kid out of jail. These days, the company supplied high-tech security for smart buildings and state-of-the-art corporate parks, competed for contracts with the most lucrative companies in the world, and owned enough patents to keep them exceedingly wealthy.

At the height of bidding on a particular project, Sebastian had been having a drink with a beautiful blonde. He hadn't known at the time she was the daughter of the man against whom they were bidding for a contract.

He'd been young, cocky, and stupid. She'd been busty, which distracted him, and extremely bright. He'd bragged they were sure to win, that nobody would come close to their number. She'd hung on him, praised him, made him feel important, and he'd admitted that they'd maxed out their bid. They couldn't go lower on their proposal. It was all the information she'd needed to grab the contract out from under them. Because of his big mouth.

Ethan blew out a harsh breath. "Fine, I didn't want it getting out that Mandy had a problem, okay? I figured the fewer people who knew, the better."

He straightened his shoulders and glared at his sibling. "You can't let it go? You were handling it as a family and didn't think I needed to be part of it? I couldn't have helped? I couldn't have been there for you?" he asked, voice rising.

"Not with something this sensitive!" Ethan shot back.

Parker rose, stepped over to Sebastian, and placed a hand on his shoulder. "Now's not the time," he told him, putting himself in between his brothers.

Glancing at Ethan, shoulders hunched, his pain obvious, Sebastian agreed. "He's right. You're hurting and you don't need to deal with this shit right now."

There'd be time for Sebastian's anger at his family later, after they'd all grieved for Mandy.

Want even more Carly books?
CARLY'S BOOKLIST by Series – visit:
http://smarturl.it/CarlyBooklist

Sign up for Carly's Newsletter:
http://smarturl.it/carlynews

Carly on Facebook:
facebook.com/CarlyPhillipsFanPage

Carly on Instagram:
instagram.com/carlyphillips

Billionaire Bad Boys Reading Order:

Book 1: Going Down Easy

Book 2: Going Down Fast

Book 3: Going Down Hard

Book 4: Going in Deep

About the Author

Carly Phillips is the *N.Y. Times* and *USA Today* Best-selling Author of over 50 sexy contemporary romance novels featuring hot men, strong women and the emotionally compelling stories her readers have come to expect and love. Carly's career spans over a decade and a half with various New York publishing houses, and she is now an Indie author who runs her own business and loves every exciting minute of her publishing journey. Carly is happily married to her college sweetheart, the mother of two nearly adult daughters and three crazy dogs (two wheaten terriers and one mutant Havanese) who star on her Facebook Fan Page and website. Carly loves social media and is always around to interact with her readers. You can find out more about Carly at www.carlyphillips.com.

Made in the USA
Coppell, TX
18 February 2020

15941913R10154